An Old English Home and Its Dependencies

S. Baring-Gould

An Old English Home and Its Dependencies

ISBN: 978-1-64799-600-0

CONTENTS

CONTENTS

iii

CHAPTER I

There lives in my neighbourhood a venerable dame, in an old bacon box in a fallen cottage, whose condition will be best understood by the annexed illustration.

Fifteen years ago the house was in habitable condition, that is to say to such as are not particular. It was true that the thatched roof had given way in places; but the proprietress obtained shelter for her head by stuffing up the chimney of the bedroom fireplace with a sack filled with chaff, and pushing her bed to the hearth and sleeping with her head under the sack.

But access to this bedroom became difficult, as the stairs, exposed to rain, rotted, and she was compelled to ascend and descend by an improvised ladder.

After a while the ladder collapsed.

Then the old lady descended for good and all, and took up her abode on the ground floor—kitchen, and parlour, and dining-room, and bedroom all in one.

"And terr'ble warm and comfortable it be," said she, when the roof fell in bodily, and covered the floor overhead.

But when the walls were exposed, rain and frost told on them, and also on the beam ends sustaining the floor, and the next stage was that one side of the floor gave way wholly.

"Tes best as it be," said the old woman; "now the rain runs off more suant."

But in falling the floor blocked the fireplace and the doorway. The consequences are—now we come to the present condition of affairs—that the old lady has had to do without a fire for certainly three winters, amongst others that bitter one of 1893-4, and her only means of egress and ingress is through the window. Of that not one half of the panes are whole; the gaps are stopped with rags.

1

And now the floor is rotted through overhead by the mouldering thatch that covers it in part, and the rain drips through.[1]

Accordingly my lady has taken refuge in an old chest, and keeps the lid up with a brick.

"Tes terr'ble cosy," says she.

Last year, having a Scottish gentleman staying with me, I took him over to call on "Marianne." We had a long interview. As we left, he turned to me with a look of dismay and said, "Good heavens! in the wildest parts of the Highlands such a thing would be impossible—and in England!"—he did not finish the sentence.

I went back to Marianne and said, "Now, tell me why you will go on living in this ruin?"

"My dear," said she, "us landed proprietors must hold on to our houses and acres. Tes a thing o' principle."

There is perhaps a margin of exaggeration in this—in speaking of acres, as I believe the said estate spreads over hardly a quarter of an acre.

How was it, and how were similar little properties acquired?

By squatting.

Formerly there was a considerable amount of common land, on which the peasants turned out their asses and geese. Then some adventuresome man, who took a wife and had no house into which to put her, annexed a piece of the common, just enough for a cottage and a garden, and none said him Nay. There was still plenty for all, and so, in time, it became his own, and was lost to the rest of the parishioners. Little by little the commons were thus encroached upon. Then, again, formerly there was much open ground by the sides of the roads. Cattle were driven along the highways often for great distances, and the turf and open spaces by the sides of the roads were provision made for their needs.

But squatters took portions of this open ground, enclosed, and built on it. There was no one to object. The lord of the manor might have

_____

[1] In the illustration the place occupied by the old woman is beneath the heap on the right hand side.

done so, but he was a little doubtful as to his right to forbid this annexation of ground on the side of the highway, and he and the parishioners generally agreed to let be. It might save the man coming on the rates if he had a garden and house—no harm was done. There was still plenty of food for the flocks and herds driven along. So we find thousands and tens of thousands of these cottages thus planted by the roadsides, with their gardens—all appropriations by squatters.

A curious thing happened to me when I was Rector of East Mersey in Essex. At the edge of the Marshes were a couple of cottages near a copious spring of limpid water. They had been built, and a tract of garden enclosed, some two hundred years ago, and occupied, rent free, by the descendants of the original appropriator. During my tenure of the rectory, the last representatives left, in fact abandoned the tenements. The Rector was lord of the manor. Accordingly these cottages, in very bad repair, fell to me, and I suddenly found myself responsible for them. Should I leave I could be come upon for dilapidations, and it would have cost me something like three hundred pounds to put these houses to right, from which I had not received a penny. Moreover, when rebuilt, no one would have rented them, so aguish and unhealthy was the spot. Accordingly I had to obtain, at some cost, a faculty to enable me to pull them down.

Some years ago Mr. Greenwood drew attention to the "North Devon Savages." These were squatters, or rather descendants of squatters, who held a piece of land and occupied a ruinous habitation, and lived in a primitive condition as to clothing and matrimonial arrangements.

A lady, who was very kind to the family, wrote to me relative to them, in 1889: "Some fifteen or sixteen years ago there was a good deal of talk about the Cheritons, or Savages as they were called. The family had been long known as worthy of this latter name, by the manner in which they lived, and their violence and depredations, real and supposed, which caused them to be regarded with a great deal of dread and almost superstitious awe. The article in the newspaper, written by a correspondent, had called attention to them, and roused their bitter resentment, and some of my menservants said that on one occasion, when they tarried from curiosity on the confines of their little property, they were almost surrounded by the family, young and old, and some almost naked,

3

with pitchforks and sticks, and that they had to continue on their way with haste. I do not know from what cause, but I think on account of some leniency he had showed them as a magistrate on one occasion, they had not as inimical a feeling towards my husband as towards the other landowners. One evening, on his return home from hunting, he told me he had heard a sad story of the head of the family, I suppose a man of thirty-eight or forty, having wounded himself badly in the foot, when shooting or poaching, and that he stoutly refused to see or have any help from clergyman or any other person; that the doctor declared it was necessary the foot should be amputated, but that the man had protested that he would sooner die as he was, and had bid him depart; that he was lying in a most miserable state. I then settled I would go to him, and if necessary stay the night there, and supposing I could persuade him to permit the operation, that I would nurse him through it, and then obtain further help. As Lord—— knew that this might be permitted by the savages, possibly, to one of his family, and as I was determined in the matter, I took a carriage and one of my little children, who could look after the horse (as it was deemed most inexpedient to have any servant with us); also all that we could think of for the comfort of an invalid; and I knew I could arrange to send back the child and trap with an escort, if I had to stay.

"When we reached that part of the road to Nymet Rowland where their field touched, we stopped, and in a moment some very angry, excited women and children rushed out. I bade them be quiet and hear what I had to say, and then told them that Lord ---- had asked me to bring these comforts to the sick man, and that I was come to offer him my services in his illness. They were instantly pacified and pleased, and begged me to come to what they called the farm—a place with half a roof and three walls. There were, I should think, three generations who lived in this place. An old woman, not altogether illiterate, the wounded man, his son, and his wife, and three or four children, and one or two sisters of his, children of the old woman.

"I did not see anything that answered to a bed there; the man was lying on two settles or sets of stools, with, I think, a blanket and something which might, or might not, have been a mattress under him.

"In order to get his head under some certain shelter, it was resting

4

on a settle in the chimney, side by side with a fire; his body and legs were on a settle in the room, if you could call a place with only three walls and half a roof by that name, and I think that the floor was in many places bare earth, and that the grass grew on it. The family were all pleasant enough—rough but grateful—and I found that though the doctor had thought amputation necessary, he now believed it might be avoided—that the man had decided against it, but allowed the doctor to continue to visit him. They were delighted with all I brought, and begged me to return soon to them, which I promised to do, and to send my children when I could not come. The old woman was a character, and quoted Scripture—certainly at random—but with some shrewdness.

"After that time I and mine were always welcome. One of the married sisters of the wounded Cheriton, who quite recovered, had bad bronchitis, and some of my family visited her continually, and on one occasion found her sitting on the thatched bit of roof, against the chimney, for 'change of air' in her convalescence. She was a big powerful woman, who had on one occasion knocked down a policeman who was taking her brother to Exeter gaol, and her mother, the old woman, told me with pride that they had had to send a cart and three men to take her away. She afterwards married a labourer. The rest of the family sold their property, and only the other day when I revisited the place for the first time after many years, I found a smart house erected in the place of the old 'Cheritons.' The women became great beggars till the death of the old mother, and the dispersion on the sale of the property.

"I remember once meeting the man Cheriton in the lane. He had decorated the collar of his horse that he was driving with horrible entrails of a sheep or pig. This was just the kind of savage ornament that would suit them.

"In the case of the woman who married the labourer, this was brought about by the Rector of Nymet, but I fancy, according to any usually received ideas, that was the one marriage; and that my use of the words wife, etc., would not stand legal interpretation."

I remember these savages between forty and fifty years ago, and then their manner of life was the same; the only clothes they wore were what they could pick from hedges where they had been put out after a wash to dry. A policeman told me he had seen one of the women in a condition of absolute nudity sitting in a hedge of their garden, suckling a child. The curate of the parish incurred their

5

resentment because he endeavoured to interfere with their primitive ways. One night, as he was riding up a lane in the dark, he thought he observed a shadow move in the darkness and steal into the hedge. Suspicious of evil, as he was near the habitation of the Cheritons, he dismounted and led his horse, and found that a gate had been taken off its hinges and laid across the way so as to throw his horse, and possibly break his neck. He at once made a dash to arrest the shadow that lurked in the hedge, but it made a bolt over the bank, and by its nakedness and fluttering rags, he was certain that the figure was that of one of the savages.

The old man, or one of the old men, finished his days—not on the paternal acres, but in a barrel littered with straw, chained to a post in an outhouse in an adjoining parish. I used him up in my story of "John Herring."

The usual end of these little holdings is that the proprietor either gets into some poaching affray, or quarrels with a neighbour, and so makes the acquaintanceship of a local lawyer, and this acquaintance leads to a loan of a little money, when the holder of the land is short of cash, on the security of the tenement. The sequel need not be further described than by saying that the property changes hands.

These are instances of paternal bits of acre rather than of acres, and such pieces are very liable to pass away, as not enough in themselves to support a family. But these are instances in small of the manner in which the manors were formed in ancient times. The manor was that estate which a man was able to get his hand upon and to hold and work through his serfs.

There is an idyllic old English home that belonged to an ancient family of the same name, the Penfounds of Penfound, in the parish of Poundstock, on the north Cornish coast.

This coast is wind-swept, yet the winds from the sea are never cold, so that wherever there is shelter there trees, shrubs, and flowers luxuriate. In a dip in the land, at the source of a little stream, snuggling into the folds of the down, bedded in foliage, open to the sun, hummed about by bees, twinkled over by butterflies, lies this lovely old house. The neighbourhood has been modernized and vulgarized distressingly, but as yet this dear old house has not been trodden out of existence. It remains on the verge of ruin, with its old hall, old garden, and stately granite doorway into the latter. A sad record belongs to this venerable manor. The family pedigree goes back to before the Wars of the Roses. The Penfounds mated with the bluest blood of the west, the Trevillians, the Kelloways, the Darells, the Pollards, the Grenvilles, the Chamonds, the Pollexfens—and the last Penfound who sat on the paternal acres died in the poorhouse of his native parish, Poundstock, in 1847, leaving issue, now poor labouring people tilling the land at so much a week—where for centuries they were manorial lords.

In ancient British times the whole country belonged to tribes, and the tribes owned their several districts. At the head of each tribe was the chief. He claimed and was given right to free maintenance by the tribesmen, and he distributed the land among the householders of the tribe. These householders owed no allegiance to any other authority than the chief, on whom they depended for everything and to whom they owed implicit obedience.

Every man who was not a tribesman was an enemy. If the tribe increased beyond what the land could maintain, it fought another tribe and wrested from it the land and drove it away or exterminated it, with complete indifference to the fact that this dispossessed tribe spoke the same tongue, had the same social organism, was of the same blood.

The tribal system from which the Celt never freed himself entirely was the curse of the Celtic race, predooming it to ruin. The history of the Welsh, the Irish, the Highlanders, is just the same as that of the Gauls, one of internecine feud, no political cohesion, no capacity for merging private interests, forgetting private grudges for a patriotic cause.

And at the bottom of all this lay the absence among the clansmen of the principle of private property. The land was possessed by all in common, subject to allotment by the chief, and among the tribal chiefs there was no link; each coveted the lands of the other. This it was which made the Celt to be everywhere a prey to such races as knew how to put self-interest in the background.

When the Jutes, Angles, Saxons, came to Britain they brought with them another social system altogether. They were possessed with the sense of the importance of private property. So deficient had the Britons been in this that they had not other than the most elementary notions of house building. Timber and wattle sufficed for them, but the Saxon, and afterwards the Norman, had a higher conception of the home, and he began at once to fashion himself a

7

permanent abode, and to make it not solid only but beautiful. And he did more than that, he brought the idea of hedges with him wherewith to enclose the land he chose to consider his own.

Saxon, Angle, or Jute put his hand down on the tribal territory, after having destroyed the tribal organization, leaving only a portion of wild moor and a tract of forest land, also a little arable land, for the members of the community whom he converted into serfs. They tilled the land, kept flocks and herds, and supplied him with what meat, wool, yarn, and grain he required; they met under his presidency in the hall at his courts. The tenants were of various sorts; some were bordarii or cotters, rendering occasional service for the use of their houses and bits of land; others, the villains, in complete servitude.

At the Norman Invasion, the Saxon thanes were themselves humbled in turn; the manors were given a more legal character and transferred to favourites of William the Conqueror. But the old Saxon chiefs in each manor were probably very rarely turned out neck and crop, but were retained as holders of the estate subject to the new lords, managing them and rendering to their masters certain dues.

In Saxon times there were book-land and folk-land, the former the private property of thanes and churls, the latter common land of the community. But after the Norman Conquest most, if not all, of the latter fell under the hand of the lord of the manor. Here and there the village community still continued to exercise its right to grant tracts to be enclosed, but usually the manorial lord claimed and exercised this right. At the present time, in my own county, this is being done in a certain parish that possessed a vast tract of common land on the confines of Dartmoor Forest. The farmers and cottagers are enclosing at a rapid rate, paying the lord of the manor a trifling fine, and thus making the land their own for ever. There can be no question that originally the fine would have gone into the parish cash-box; now it goes into the landlord's pocket.

"There is much that is primitive and simple to be met with, but nothing of barbarism in the land institutions of Saxon England, unless, indeed, an excessive love for it, and an almost exaggerated deference for its possession may be so classed. In an age when freedom was the exceptional condition, the ownership of land was the mark of a free man, and ample territory the inseparable appanage of rank. No amount of gold or chattel property conferred the franchise: land alone was recognized as the vehicle of all personal privilege, and the basis of civil rank. Centuries have not obliterated these features in their descendants to this day; the love of land, its estimation above all other forms of property, and its political preponderance."[2]

Reformers have roundly abused, and striven to break down our land system, especially the right of primogeniture, and to resolve the land into small holdings to be cultivated by small owners. There are, as in all social and political questions, two sides to this. I do not deny for a moment that much is to be said in favour of equal partition of land among all the children, and of the multiplication of peasant proprietors. But I venture to think that the system that has prevailed in England has produced results that could have been attained by no other. In this especially, that it has provided at once a stable core, with a body of fluid, migratory, and energetic young people, who have not been bound to the clod.

A man, knowing that his land will descend to his son and son's son, will plant and improve, and spend his money most unselfishly on the land, for the family advantage. But if he thinks that it will go into other hands, will he for this purpose deny himself present luxuries and amusements?

I suppose such an alternative as this has presented itself to many a landowner. "I ought to spend from £150 to £200 in planting this autumn. Shall I do it, or run up to town, go to the opera, eat, drink, and enjoy myself, and spend the money on myself?"

There is, surely, something very beautiful and wholesome in the manner in which an Englishman of means lives for, and cares for the family, as a whole—the generations unborn, as well as his own children—and builds, plants, provides for the future, furnishing it with a lovable centre, from which it may radiate into all lands.

It was, unless I am greatly mistaken, the principle of equal subdivision, or of gavelkind, that existed among the Welsh, which ruined their cause. The Celt has more originality, genius, energy than the Saxon, but he was paralyzed in his attempts to resist the invader by the interminable break-up of power and of property at the death of every prince. The kinglet of Glamorgan had ten sons—

[2] Wren Hoskins, in Systems of Land Tenure in Various Countries, London, 1870, p. 100.

9

one became a monk, and the rest parcelled up his lands and his authority over men. A great prince like Howel Dda was able to consolidate the nation, but only for his lifetime; at his death it was torn into petty factions by his sons. It was this that maimed the Briton before the Saxon, not the superiority in genius, numbers, character in the latter; and it was this again which threw Wales at the feet of the Norman kings.

Now look at almost all the farm-buildings in France. Everything there is in ruin, all the outward tokens of decay are manifest. Why is this? Because no owner cares to spend money on putting the place to rights. Everything will be divided at his death, and he must hoard his money for division among those children who do not take the farm. So one gets a tumble-down tenement, and the rest the money that might make it habitable. Moreover, this continued to the next generation ends in the disappearance of the family from its paternal acres. In the Limousin there is hardly a family that retains its hold on its land over the third generation.

I know four delightful old ladies, all unmarried, inheriting a well-known and honoured name in Perigord. On the fathers death everything was divided. One took the château, without having the money to repair it, and she lives under the ruins. The second took a farm and lives with the paysan and paysanne. The third took the family plate and china and family portraits, and lives over a modiste in small lodgings, and is obliged to sell her ancestral goods piecemeal to keep herself going. The fourth took some shares the father had in a Pâté de Foix gras factory; it failed, and she has to scramble on upon the alms of her sisters.

Among the peasants the tenure of small holdings is mischievous; they are chained to the soil, whereas, if set free, they might emigrate and become energetic colonists, or go into the towns and become intelligent, active artisans. It is just when a young man ought to be starting on a career that he acquires a few acres, and at once he is paralyzed. Those acres hold him, he cannot do justice to them, he has not the means. He does not like to part with them, and he spends his life bowed over them. Worse than this, unable to avert the further dismemberment of his estate on his death, he resolves in compact with his wife to have no more than one, or at the most two children. Now, with us, the younger son of a landed proprietor knows he must push his way in the world, and from the moment his intelligence begins to act he looks about him for openings. Our labourers also, unchained to the soil, go about wherever work may be had. Where there is a market for their abilities, thither they go, but go they would not, if they owned their little plot of land and house.

And, if I am not much mistaken, it is this early developed sense of independence that has been the making of Englishmen all over the world; but, then, it is the conservative element, the holding to the paternal acres, that has made of dear old England one great garden and park, the proprietor spending his money on the land, instead of on his pleasures or self, as elsewhere.

CHAPTER II

As every circle has its centre, so had every manor its hall, the centre of its organization, the heart whence throbbed the vital force through the district, and to which it returned. The hall was not merely the place where the lord lived, for he did not always occupy it, but it was the gathering place of the courts leet and baron.

It is the fashion to hold that land was originally held in common, and that private proprietorship in land is an encroachment on the public rights.

That was, no doubt, the case with the Celt, and it has been fatal to his ever taking a lead among the nations; it has so eaten into his habits of mind as to have rendered him incapable of being other than a subject under the control of another people, which had happily got beyond such infantile notions.

It is the case with individuals, starting on the battle of life, that they sometimes, by chance, take a wrong direction, and then, once involved therein, have not the power or will or chance to turn back and take another. That is how some men make a botch of their lives, whereas others, perhaps their inferiors in ability, by mere accident strike on a course which leads to power, prosperity, and a name.

It is so among nations, races—and among these the highly-gifted Celt went wrong at the outstart, and that is it which has been his bane through centuries. Now the time for recovery is past. He is forced to take a lower room.

The French, that is to say the Gauls under Frank domination, were forcibly put right. I do not deny that feudalism led to gross abuses, and that it was well to have these swept away, but that which I think was fatal to France at the Revolution was reversion to the Celtic principle of subdivision. This is inevitably and inexorably killing France; it is reducing its population, extinguishing its life.

Between 1831 and 1840 there were in France but three departments in which the mortality exceeded the natality, now there are between forty-five to sixty departments in this condition.

"If we traverse France rapidly in train from the Channel to the Pyrenees, there is one observation that may be made from the carriage windows. Between the Loire and the Garonne, in departments where the soil is poor, there the houses are smiling and well kept—there is evidence of comfort. But, on the contrary, in the departments formerly the richest, there are crumbling walls and empty houses.... The rich departments are being depopulated, and in the poor ones there the population remains stationary or only slowly decreases."[3]

The population in the rich departments is dwindling at the rate of 50 per cent. in half a century.

Why is this? Because all property is subdivided. In the poor districts, too, land will not support all those born, and therefore some take up trades or go as labourers and artisans.

The increase in population in France per thousand in the year is 18, whereas in Prussia it is 13.

I was much amused last summer with the remark of a little fellow of twelve, who was showing me the way across some fields, as a short cut. I remarked on the beauty of the place, and the fertility of the soil. "Yes," said he, "but I think it is time for me to be moving, and look out for some place for myself."

Such a thought, springing up in an English child's mind, would not occur to a French child. But it is just this which has made us successful colonists, and it is the absence of this which makes French colonies dead failures. Whereas we and the Germans pour forth tens of thousands of emigrants, France sends to her North African Settlements just over six hundred persons per annum—and they are nearly all officials.

The maker of pottery, after having tempered his clay, puts into it particles of grit, of sand, and about these the clay crystallizes, and it is the making these centres of crystallization that gives to pottery its cohesion. Without these particles it goes to pieces in burning, it breaks up with the least pressure. And our manor houses are these particles of grit, centres of crystallization to our people, that make us so tough and so cohesive a race—at least, I think it is one very important element in the manufacture.

---

[3] Dumont, "La dépopulation," in Revue de l'École d'Anthropologie, Jan., 1897.

If we desire to study the organization of a manor as set about by one of the branches of the great Scandinavian-Teutonic stock, we cannot do better than observe the conduct of the settlers in Iceland at the end of the ninth century.

When the Norsemen came to Iceland they brought with them their thralls, and they proceeded to make their claims to land, till they had portioned out all the soil worth having among the great heads of families. The land thus fell into shares, such as we should call manors, and each share was under a chief, who planted on the soil his kinsmen, and any others who applied to him for allotments. No freeman, if he could help it, would accept the land as a gift, for the reception of a gift entailed responsibility to the giver, a sort of dependence that the free spirit of the race greatly disliked.

"The period during which the settlement of Iceland was going on lasted about sixty years. At the end of that time the island was as fully peopled as it has ever been since. During all that period each chief, and his children after him, had lived on his holding, which proved a little kingdom of itself, allotting his land to new comers, whose kinship, turn of mind, or inferiority in rank allowed them to accept the gift, marrying and inter-marrying with the families of neighbouring chiefs, setting up his children in abodes of their own, putting his freed men and thralls out in farms and holdings, fulfilling the duties of the priesthood in his temple, and otherwise exercising what we should call the legitimate influence on those around him, to which he was entitled by his strength of arm, or birth, or wealth."[4]

This is just what took place in the conquest of Britain by the Saxons, Jutes, and Angles. They portioned out the land among them, and turned the original inhabitants into serfs; to some of these they gave tenements to hold subject to service: these are now represented by our tenant farmers; to others, kinsmen, they gave lands free of charge, but under their own lordship: such are the ancestors of our yeomen.

Now an Icelandic chief was magistrate and priest in one. He was called the Godi—the Good man. Hard by his hall was the sacred circular temple, and he offered sacrifice therein. In his hall were assembled the free householders, to consult relative to the affairs of the district. This was the husting, or house council. We had

---

4 Dasent, History of Brunt Nial, 1861, vol. i. p. xiv.

precisely the same condition of affairs in England. Where a manor is there is the hall, and in that hall were held the courts, which all free holders attended.

Very probably each Anglo-Saxon lord had his temple adjoining his hall, but when England became Christian, several manors, when small, combined to keep a priest between them; but when the church adjoins the manor house, then almost certainly it occupies the site of the old heathen Saxon temple; except in Wessex, which was subjugated by Christianised Saxons.

The hall was the social and political centre of each community. There the lord showed hospitality, administered justice, appointed his thralls their tasks, and received the dues of his tenants.

In the earliest period, in it he and his house-churls and family slept, as well as ate and worked. But the women had a separate apartment, which in time became the with-drawing room. Bedrooms, kitchens, parlours, were aftergrowths, as men sought more comfort or privacy, and these were grouped about the hall. Nevertheless, the custom of sleeping in the hall continued till Tudor times.

It is instructive to notice the difference between the residence of the feudal lord on the Continent and that occupied by him in England. In the former his place of abode is a castle, château, derived from castellum, schloss, from schliesen, a place into which the lord might lock himself in and from whence lock out all enemies. But the English terms—mansion, manor-house, hall, court, imply nothing military, give token of no exclusiveness, make no threat. The chronic warfare and petty disturbances that prevailed on the continent of Europe obliged the lords of the soil to perch their residences on inaccessible and barren rocks, whereas in England they are seated comfortably in valleys, in the midst of the richest land. In France, in Germany, in Italy, each feudal owner quarrelled with his neighbour, and made war on him when he listed. There was nothing of that kind in England. With the exception of the struggle between Stephen and Matilda, and the Wars of the Roses, we were spared serious internecine strife, and the hand of the king was strong enough to put down private feuds.

The castle was an importation into England, brought in by the Norman and Angevin kings, and it was only the foreign favourites to whom the king granted vast numbers of manors who had castles.

But the castles never affectedEnglish domestic architecture; on the contrary, the English sense of comfort, peace, and goodwill prevailed over the fortress, broke holes in it for immense windows and for wide doorways; and nothing remained of menace and power except the towers and battlements.

On the Continent, however, till the eighteenth century, the type of fortress prevailed; the angle towers became turrets, but were indispensable wherever a gentleman had a château. As to the English noble or squire, his only tower was the dove-cot, and the holes in it not for muskets and crossbows, but for the peaceful pigeon to fly in and out.

The pedigree of a castle is this:

The stronghold in France in Merovingian days consisted of an adaptation of the Roman camp. It was an earthwork with a stockade on top, enclosing a level tract on the top of a hill, if a suitable hill could be found; within was a mound, a motte; on this stood a great round tower of woodwork, in which lived the chief. The earthwork surrounding the camp had mounds at intervals, and in the space within the stockade were similar constructions, a hall and storehouses.

Now the mediæval castle was precisely this, with the one exception—that stone took the place of wood, and the tower on a mound became the keep.

When the Normans came to England they translated to our island the type of castle they had been accustomed to in France. They had to bring their architects, in some cases their material, from France. But, whereas this became the type of the château in France, it had nothing to do with the genesis of the manor-house in old England. Our manor-houses did not pass out of lordly castles, but out of halls. The very situation of our old manorial mansions shows that they were never thought of as fortresses.

The Anglo-Saxon did no building of domestic architecture save with wood. The English lord lived in his great wooden hall, with his tenants and bonders about him. If he squeezed them, it was gently, as a man milks his cow. Of the Norman it was said, Quot domini castellorum, tot tyranni.

In France the fortress of the peasant was the church, and the tower

16

his keep, and in times of trouble he conveyed his goods to the church, and the entire building became to him a city of refuge. That is why wells, bake-houses, and other conveniences are found in connection with many foreign churches.

The battlements of our churches and their towers may perhaps point to these having been regarded in something the same light by the inhabitants of a parish in England, but more probably they came into use when the roofs were not steep, and instead of being slated or shingled, were covered with lead. To a lead roof, a parapet is necessary, or rather advisable; and the parapet not only finishes it off above the wall, but also serves to conceal the ugliness of a low-pitched roof. And the parapet was broken into battlements to enable the gutter to be readily cleaned, by throwing over accumulations of snow and leaves.

The battlement became a mere ornament—almost a joke to English architects; they even battlemented the transoms of windows, and the caps of pillars. It would seem as though, in the sense of security in which the English were, they took a pleasure in laughing at the grave precautions employed on the Continent, where the battlement was something far too serious and important to be treated as an ornament.

The poor old hall has shrunk and been degraded into a mere lobby, in which to hang up great coats and hats and sticks and umbrellas. Originally it was the main feature of the manor-house, to which everything else was subsidiary; then it was ceiled over, a floor put across it, and it became a reception-room, and now a reception-room for overcoats only.

But let it be borne in mind where a real hall is in place and where it is not. It belongs to a manor and to a manor only; it is incongruous in a villa residence, and wholly out of place in a town dwelling. Many a modern gentleman's place in the country is designed to look very pretty and very mediæval or Tudor; but this is all so much ornament stuck on, and the organic structure agreeth not therewith.

The hall, so far from excluding people, was so open-doored as to invite not people only but all the winds of heaven to blow into and through it.

Very usually the front door of the house under the porch opened into it, and immediately opposite was the door out of the hall into the court. Naturally the wind marched through.

17

As a bit of shelter a screen was run up, but only of timber, and the passage boxed in. Above was the minstrels' gallery; and in the screen were, of course, doors into the hall, and a buttery hatch, as on the further side of the passage was either kitchen or cellar, or both.

To almost every hall was a slit or eye and earlet hole communicating with a lady's chamber. The tyrant Dionysius of Syracuse had a prison which was so constructed that every whisper in it from one prisoner to another was carried through a tube to his private apartment, where he sat and listened to what his captives said.

The slit above mentioned was the Dionysius's ear of that domestic tyrant, the lady of the house. She sat in her room, with her ear to this opening, when her good lord revelled and joked in the hall with his boon companions, and afterwards—behind the curtains—his words were commented on and his jokes submitted to searching criticism. Moreover, through this slit her eye raked the hall when the servants were there, and she could see if they attended to their work or romped with the men, or idled gossiping.

We have so far advanced that the ear is no longer employed—but the domestic tyrant is, I am credibly informed, still with us, advancing triumphant through ages, and like a snowball acquiring force, consistency, and hardness in progress.

CHAPTER III

In 1891 I was excavating a village at the edge of Trewortha Marsh, on the Bodmin Moors, in Cornwall. There were a number of oblong huts, but one seemed to have been occupied by more than one family, as it was divided into stalls, by great slabs of granite set up on edge, and in front of each stall was a hearth on the soil, and the soil burnt brick-red from heat.

The pottery found strewn about was all wheel-turned, but early and rude, and no trace of glass could be found. These habitationsbelonged to a period after the Roman invasion, and probably to Britons.

The hearth is the centre of family life, what the hall is to the manor. About it gather all who are bound together by community of blood and interest, and this is still recognized, for it is counted an unwarrantable presumption in a stranger to poke your fire.

But how small and degenerate is our fire from what it once was. Coal having taken the place of logs, the hearth has been reduced and the grate has supplanted the dogs or andirons, and the gaping fireplace is closed in.

I know an old Elizabethan mansion where the chimney-stack containing three flues descends into the hall and has in it three fireplaces, so that simultaneously three fires could burn in the same room, and the family circle could fold about the three hearths combined into one in an almost complete circle.

And what chimneys those were in old times! Bacon-sides were hung in them, so large were they, and not infrequently a ladder could be put up them to communicate with a little door that gave access to a secret place.

I was looking not long ago at the demolition of a good yeoman's dwelling in Cornwall. By the side of the hearth, opening into the kitchen-hall, was a walled-up door, against which usually a dresser or cupboard stood. This walled-up door communicated with a goodly chamber or cellar formed in the thickness of the chimney, and without an opening to the light outside. Access to this chamber could, however, always be had by means of a hand-ladder placed when required in the chimney. This admitted through a door in the chimney to the receptacle for kegs—for that was the real purpose of the concealed place, it was the yeoman's cellar of spirits that had never paid customs. When a fresh supply was taken in, the door into the kitchen was unwalled and the cellar filled with kegs, then walled up again and plastered over. But as spirits were wanted they were got by means of the ladder—keg by keg.

It was in such a chamber in the wall, to which access was alone obtainable through the chimney, that Garnet and Oldcorne were concealed after the Gunpowder Plot. This is how Ainsworth describes the place of retreat: "Mrs. Abindon conducted the two priests to one of the large fireplaces. A raised stone about two feet high occupied the inside of the chimney, and upon it stood an immense pair of iron dogs. Obeying Mrs. Abindon's directions, Garnet got upon the stone, and setting his foot on the large iron knob on the left, found a few projections in the masonry on the side, up which he mounted, and opening a small door made of planks of wood, covered with bricks and coloured black, so as not to be distinguishable from the walls of the chimney, crept into a recess contrived in the thickness of the wall. This cell was about two feet wide and four high, and was connected with another chimney at the back by means of three or four small holes. Across its sides ran a narrow stone shelf, just wide enough to afford an uncomfortable seat."

But these wide chimneys, if they allowed ascent, also permitted descent, and many a house was entered and burgled by this means.

There was in my own neighbourhood, about a century ago, a man who lived in a cave above the Tamar, in Dunterton Wood, whose retreat was known to none, and who was a terror to the neighbourhood. He was wont during the night to visit well-to-do persons' houses within reach, get over the roof to the chimney of the hall, and descend it. Once in the house he collected what he listed, unbarred the door, and walked away with his spoil.

So great was the terror inspired by this man in the neighbourhood that all householders who had anything to lose had spiked contrivances of iron put into their chimneys, so that the burglar in descending at a rapid pace stood a chance of being impaled. The other day, in repairing my hall chimney, I came on this contrivance.

The end of the man was this. Colonel Kelly, of Kelly, was out one day with his pack of foxhounds, when they made a set at the cave, and so it was discovered with the man in it and a great accumulation of plunder. I believe he was hung.

The same cave was employed as a place of refuge for an escaped convict some fifty years ago. After that, the late Mr. Kelly blew up the cave with gunpowder, and its place is now occupied by the ruins of the rock above. It can conceal no more lawbreakers.

There was something very pleasant in the old evening round the great fire. If one of wood, then, in a farmhouse, the grandfather in the ingle-corner was an indispensable feature. A wood fire requires constant attention, and it was his place to put the logs together as they burnt through; and he knew he was useful, and when the farmer's wife or his granddaughter came to the hearth for a bit of cooking she had always a pleasant word for the old man.

The settle was another feature.

There is a species much used formerly in Somersetshire and Devon, and perhaps elsewhere. It was a multum-in-parvo. The back opened and disclosed a place in which sides of bacon were hung. Above was a long narrow cupboard for the groceries. The seat lifted—for what think you? As a place where the baby could be placed in greatest security whilst the mother was engaged at the fire. I believe that dealers now call them monks' seats. Monks' seats! they belonged to women and babies. But a dealer knows how to humbug his customers.

I was once in a certain county, I will not say which, and visited a gentleman who had bought and built a fine house, very modern, but very handsome. Then the fancy took him to be possessed of old oak, so he went to a dealer.

"My dear sir," said Lazarus, "I have the very thing for you—a superb antique oak mantelpiece and sideboard—the finest in England of the date of Henry VIII. But they are all in an ancient mansion, a black-timbered hall in Cheshire or Shropshire—I forget which. Would you care to go down and see it? The house is to be pulled down, and I must remove the contents."

Of course Mr. Greenhorn went, bought all at a fabulous price, and brought them to his mansion. Well, anyone with the smallest knowledge of old oak would see at a glance that this was all Belgian stuff, made up of bits from old churches, put together higgledy-piggledy without any unity of design—stuff that no ancient would have designed, for there was no design in it. And the dealer kept this Cheshire or Shropshire black-timbered house regularly supplied with this detestable rubbish, and regularly took greenhorns to it to pay down heavy gold for what was worth nothing but a few Belgian francs.

At the risk of branching away from my topic, I must have another word relative to dealers.

There is still in England a good deal of good plain old oak; old cradles, old standing clock cases, old bureaus, etc., without any carving on them, but fine in their lines and in their simplicity. These wretches buy them up and give them into the hands of mechanical carvers to adorn in "Elizabethan style," and then they sell these good old articles of furniture—defaced and spoiled and rendered all but worthless.

"Good heavens!" said I to one of these gentry; "you have utterly, irrevocably ruined that noble wardrobe."

"Well, sir, I couldn't sell it for one-tenth of the price hadn't I done this. The buyers like this, and I have to suit their taste."

To return to the hearth and to the settle.

A friend one day saw a screen of carved oak in a cottage. He bought it for half a guinea, and then called me into consultation on it. With a little study it revealed itself to be the back of a settle of Henry VII.'s reign. The mortices for the arms and for the seat were there; also nail marks showing that stamped leather had been fastened to the back below the sculpture. There were pegs showing where had been the pilasters sustaining the canopy, and one scrap of canopy still extant. I show the restoration (p. 57).

Fine though this be, I know something better still—not in art, but for cosiness, and that is the curved settle, it is constructed in an arc. In a farmhouse I know well are two such settles, and they are connected by a curved iron rod fastened to the ceiling, and there are green baize curtains depending from this rod.

On a winter evening, the farmer and his wife and the serving maidens and young men come into the kitchen, and the circle is completed with chairs or stools, the curtains are drawn, the fire is made up, and a very jolly evening is spent with cakes and cider, and tales and jokes and song.

I was at a sale one day—a very small farm but an old one. A farmer bid for the settle—a small one. One of his daughters was there. She turned to her sister and said: "I say, Nan, vaither he've gone and bought the settle, and it's lovely; it will hold only two."

"Well, Jane," said her sister, "I reckon—that depends. You must have the right one beside y'; then it's just large enough, and you don't want no more."

When I was a child, some sixty years ago, the mat before the fire was the line of demarcation, beyond which a youngster might not go.

"My dear," said my grandmother, "fires are made to be seen—not felt."

Oh, how we shivered beyond the mat! I used to look at a patent bacon-toaster, and resolve, when I was a man and independent, to have a curved settle formed of burnished tin, and to sit before a roaring fire in the focus of all the converging rays, and never stir therefrom from Michaelmas till Lady Day. But the curved settle answers the purpose.

Among the troubles and irritations of life, one of the worst is a smoky chimney, and among all the hideousness of modern contrivances nothing surpasses the cowl.

It is very curious that architects should set themselves to work to violate first principles, and so involve us in these troubles. In the first place, to ensure that a chimney shall not smoke, the flue must be made large enough to carry the smoke. This is a principle very generally neglected. Next it is necessary that the chimney should not have a flat top, for then the wind beats against the broad surface, and, of course, prevents the smoke from rising, and much of it is deflected down the flue.

What our forefathers did was to reduce the top to a thin edge that could not arrest and drive the smoke down, but would, on the contrary, assist it in rising. Or else they covered over the orifice with a roof, open at the sides, that prevented the wind from descending, and enabled the smoke to get away whichever way the wind blew.

In order to illustrate what I mean, I have simply taken my pencil and gone outside my house, and have drawn an old and a new chimney-top.

The chimney-piece or overmantel is the reredos of the family altar, and should contain the arms of the family or the portraits of ancestors.

No portion of an old manor-house was so decorated and enriched as this; and the hall fireplace received pre-eminent attention.

Happily we have in England numerous and splendid examples; but a vast number were sacrificed at the end of last century and the beginning of the present, when large looking-glasses came into fashion, and to make place for them the glorious old sculptured wood was ruthlessly torn down. If the reader is happy enough to possess a copy of Dr. Syntax's Tours, he will see the period of transition. In the second Tour is a plate representing the doctor visiting the Widow Hopefull at York. The room is panelled with oak, the ceiling is of plaster beautifully moulded, the chimney-piece is of oak carved, but painted over, and the large open hearth has been closed in, reduced, and a little grate inserted.

In the same volume is a picture of Dr. Syntax making his will. Here the large open fireplace remains, lined with Dutch tiles, and the fire is on dogs. All the lower portion of the mantel decoration remains, but above the shelf everything has been removed to make way for the mirror.

In the same volume is Dr. Syntax painting a portrait, and here again is a lovely panelled room with plaster ceiling and a simple but charming chimney-piece of excellent design.

Now turn to the first Tour, and look at Dr. Syntax mistaking a gentleman's house for an inn. Here we have the chimney-piece supported on vulgar corbels, all of the period when Rowlandson drew; above the shelf is a painting in the worst description of frame. When Rowlandson made his drawings, he was absolutely incapable of appreciating Gothic design, and whenever he attempted this he failed egregiously, but the feeling for what was later, Elizabethan and Jacobean, was by no means dead in him, and he drew the details with a zest that shows he loved the style.

CHAPTER IV

To my taste old furniture in a modern jerry-built villa residence is as out of place as modern gim-crack chairs and tables and cabinets in an ancient mansion. In the first instance you have solidly constructed furniture in a case that is thin, and not calculated to last a century. With regard to the second, happily we have now excellently designed furniture, well constructed on old models; and what I mean by gim-crack stuff is that which was turned out by upholsterers to within the last fifteen years.

Look at the construction of a chair, and see what I mean.

Full well do I recall the introduction into my father's house of these chairs. Only a fragment of one now remains. Observe the legs; they curve out below, and are as uncalculated to resist the pressure downward of a heavy person sitting on them, as could well be contrived. Then again the braces—look at them; they are spindles with the ends let into holes drilled half-way through the legs. Old braces were braces, these are mere sources of weakness, they do not brace; when weight is applied to the seat the tendency is to drive the legs apart, then out falls the brace. No mortice holds it, it has no function to fulfil. In the old chair how firm all the joints are made! Stout oak pegs are driven throughevery mortice, and every precaution is taken to prevent gaping at the joints, to resist strain put on them.

Mention has been made of the great looking-glass, which was the occasion of the destruction of so many carved chimney-pieces. There was another introduction, and that into the drawing-room, which produced a disfiguring effect, and that was the large circular rosewood table.

At the beginning of this century it entered our parlour, settled there, and made the room look uncomfortable. By no arrangement of the furniture could the drawing-room be given a cosy look. The table got in the way of visitors, it prevented the formation of pleasant groups; it was a very barrier to friendship, and a block to conversation.

25

One evening, in the South of France, I received intimation from a M. Dols, avocat, that he would be pleased to receive me. I had sent word to him before that I should like to call on him and see some interesting flint swords and celts in his possession. He asked me to call in the evening at 8 p.m. Accordingly I went to his door, and was ushered into the salon. The centre was occupied by a table, of considerable size, and the family was seated beyond the table.

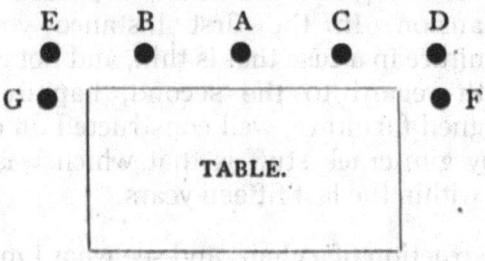

M. Dols occupied B; Mme. Dols occupied C; M. Dols' mother was planted at D; and the maiden sister of Mme. Dols at E. M. Gaston Dols, the son, was at G, and Mlle. Eulalie Dols, the daughter, at F. The chair A was left vacant for the visitor.

But conceive the situation! To be introduced like a criminal before six judges, then, when one had reached the seat allotted, to be planted one in a row, and to have to distribute remarks right and left; to address the ancestress at D across the shirtfront of M. Dols at B, and to say something pretty to the old maid at E athwart the swelling bosom of Mme. Dols at B!

If only that detestable table could have been got rid of, we would have gravitated together into a knot and been happy—but to be lively and chatty in espalier was impossible.

Well! it was almost as bad in the old days, when we had large round tables in our drawing-rooms; and one of the great achievements of modern—I mean quite recent—times has been the bundling of that old rosewood table out. That gone, the rest of the furniture gets together into comfortable groups, and everything finds its place. Before, all were overawed and sent to the wall in deference to the round table.

A word or two is due to the chest of drawers. This, I conceive, is a development of the old oak chest, in which the valuables, or the linen, or the sundry garments of the family were kept. Countless specimens of these oak chests remain; some very fine, some plain. There is, moreover, the spruce chest, made of cypress wood, that was thought to preserve silk and cloth from the moth. Oak chests are usually carved, more or less; cypress chests are sketched over with red-hot iron.

Now there was an inconvenience in the chest. A hasty and untidy person turned its contents upside down to find what he or she particularly wanted, and which was, of course, at the bottom. If the husband did this, he had words cast at him that made him miserable for the rest of the day.

So it was clearly advisable that husband and wife and each child should have a separate chest. But that did not suffice; one was needed for bed linen, one for table linen, a third for personal linen. The result would have been an accumulation of chests, when, happily, the notion struck someone that drawers would solve the difficulty. Let the top of the chest remain immovable, and break up the front into parallel strips, each strip having a drawer behind it.

An old chest of drawers can be known by the way in which the drawers are made to run. They have a groove let into their sides corresponding with a strip of oak or runner on each side of the case; thus they do not rest the one on the other, but on their runners. When each drawer was separately cased in, then the need for runners came to an end.

It is deserving of observation how slowly and cautiously our forefathers multiplied the drawers. At first, two were thought quite as many as could be ventured upon, but after about a century the makers grew bolder and multiplied them.

Does it chance that there be a reader of this chapter who possesses a cupboard, partly open in front, with small balustrades in the door between which the contents of the cupboard can be seen? If he or she has, ten to one but it has been converted into a receptacle for china, or glass, and then china and glass are not only imperfectly exhibited, but become rapidly covered with dust. The possessor of such a little cabinet or cupboard owns something now become very rare, the significance of which is understood by a few only.

Let me describe one in my possession. The height is two feet eight inches, by two feet one inch, and the depth eight and a half inches. There are two doors in front: the upper is perforated and has eight little balustrades in it; the lower door is solid; but this lower door, instead of engrossing the entire front of the cabinet, is small, six inches square, and occupies one compartment of the three, into which the lower portion of the front is divided. Each door gives access to a separate compartment.

Now, what is this droll little article of furniture? What was its original use?

When I answer that it was a livery cupboard, I have little doubt that the majority of my readers will think, as did someone I know who asked about it and received this answer, that it was intended for livery badges—the metal plates with coats of arms engraved on them—worn anciently by servants upon their left arms in a nobleman's and gentleman's household.

But no. A livery cupboard had not this signification. It was the cupboard in which was kept that portion of food and of wine or ale delivered over to each person in the household by the lady of the house for night consumption. Anciently—in the days of Good Queen Bess and of James I.—there was no meal between supper at 7 p.m. and breakfast at 10 a.m., and when each person retired for the night he or she carried off a portion of food, served out, if not by the hands of the hostess, then under her eye; and this "delivery" was carried upstairs to the bedroom and was stowed away in the cupboard appropriated to its use, that on waking in the night, or early in the morning for a hunt or a hawking, or a journey, the food and refreshing draught might be handy, and stay the stomach till all met for the common meal served in the hall at ten o'clock.

We still speak of livery stables, but this does not mean that there coachmen and grooms who wear livery attend to horses, but that the horses themselves receive there their livrée—delivery of so many feeds of oats. This is made clear enough by a passage in Spenser's account of the state of Ireland, written in the middle of the sixteenth century. He says: "What livery is, we by common use in England know well enough, namely, that it is an allowance of horse-meat; as they commonly use the word stabling, as to keep horses at livery; the which word, I guess, is derived of livering or delivering forth their nightly food; so in great houses, the livery is said to be served up for all night—that is, their evening allowance for drink."

Another reference to the custom of serving liveries for all night is made by Cavendish in his Life of Wolsey, where, in giving a description of the Cardinal's Embassy to Charles V. at Bruges, he says: "Also the Emperor's officers every night went through the town, from house to house, where as many Englishmen lay or resorted, and there served their liveries for all night, which was done in this manner: first, the Emperor's officers brought into the house a cake of fine manchet bread, two great silver pots, with wine, and a pound of fine sugar; white lights and yellow; a bowl or goblet of silver to drink in; and every night a staff torch. This was the order of their liveries."

These little livery cupboards usually stood on another, from which they were detached, and which was the "court-cupboard." In this the inmate of the room kept his valuables.

Now let me bid my readers keep a sharp eye on the furniture of cottages when theyvisit them, for these livery cupboards may still be occasionally found in them, and then they go by the name of "bread and cheese cupboards." I remember many years ago picking up one in a labourer's cottage, that was used for cheese, and it did not lose this smell for a long time afterwards.

But these livery cupboards may also be seen in some churches where doles of bread are given on certain days; and in them, under lock and key, the loaves remain on the day of distribution till given away.

As already intimated, these livery cupboards are now scarce, and it behoves anyone who has one such to treasure it, and anyone who can procure such a cupboard to get it.

There is another cupboard that should be valued—the dear old corner-cupboard. This also has a pedigree.

It was not always put in the corner. Its proper place was in the dining-room, and there it contained the conserves, the distilled waters, the home-made wines that testified to the skill of the housewife. It contained more than that—the nutmegs, the cinnamon, the mace, the pepper, all the precious spices that came from the blessed islands over the sea, and were costly and highly esteemed. In most dining-rooms of the reign of Charles II. or Queen Anne, this cupboard will be found let into the wall, usually arched over above, a necessary adjunct to the room; and when the bowl of punch had to be brewed the lady of the house unlocked it, and at once the whole room was pervaded with fragrance as from the spice isles.

29

Who among us who are getting old do not recall the peculiar curranty savour of the ancient dining-room? I have a white-haired uncle—he will forgive my telling it—who, when I was a child, and he a young man from Oxford, invariably sought opportunities, and found them, for getting at such a cupboard, and filling his hand first, and then his mouth, with currants. To this day, I never see him without a waft of that old corner-cupboard coming over me.

And the stout and ruddy yeoman, as he dipped the whalebone and silver ladle into the steaming bowl, in which floated circles of lemon, sang:

> "Behold the wealthy merchant, that trades on foreign seas,
> And brings home gold and treasure, for such as live at ease,
> With spices and with cinnamon, and oranges also,
> They're brought us from the Indies, by the virtue of the plough."

Then came the reign of the Georges, when men built for show rather than for comfort, and the walls were of thin brick overlaid with composition to keep the rain out; and the composition was covered with oil-paint to keep the rain out of the cracks in the plaster and in the bricks. In such houses there were no deep walls in which cupboards could lurk. It was necessary to have cupboards and cabinets made as detached pieces of furniture, taking up room, giving us knocks when we inadvertently run against them; and these cupboards and cabinets were of veneered stuff, common wood underneath, with a thin film of mahogany or rosewood glued on, and every knock given struck off a bit of veneer, and a change of weather scaled off pieces, and gave the whole a shabby, measly look. Then to get her precious cupboard out of the way of being knocked, and thereby her bottles of liqueurs and syrups being knocked over, the lady of the house devised the corner-cupboard.

Also, as things Chinese and Japanese and Indian were much in fashion, these cupboards in the corner were very generally painted dark green or black, and were ornamented with raised gold figures— all in imitation of Oriental flowers and birds and men, and very generally were furnished with beautiful brass-work locks and hinges.

Nearly every old house has its secret cupboard—usually in the wall. Very often one may be found behind the panelling, and near the fire. In my own house is one cut in granite, the stone on all sides, and is the depth of my arm. I have little doubt that these warm, dry cupboards, so secured that no mouse can make its way in, were for the preservation of deeds. Others were for jewellery and plate. The custom of having secret cupboards was continued after cupboards had become independent articles of furniture, standing out in the room; but then they took the form of secret compartments, not opened by keys, but by moving some part of the moulding, or by pressure on some ornamental plate or piece of inlaid wood or ivory.

It is said that everyone has his secret closet, and that in it everyone has his skeleton. I do not know much about the cupboards of nowaday folk, but when I think of those I knew in the olden times, it seems to me that they were full of nothing other than sweets and spices, of gold and gems; anyhow, such were the cupboards of our grandmothers, our maiden aunts, and our great-grandmothers. And when we chance in some secret compartment to light on a bundle of their letters, and look into them, then it is just like the opening of their corner-cupboards, out pours a sweet and spicy fragrance—that of the generous thoughts and kind wishes of their dear old honest and God-fearing hearts.

CHAPTER V

When I was a small boy at King's College School, I boarded with one of the masters, at a corner house in Queen's Square. There was a long room in which we boarders—there were some five-and-twenty of us—had our meals, and prepared lessons for the morrow in the evening, under the supervision of an usher.

One day at tea, the usher having been summoned out of the room, we boys essayed who could throw up his piece of bread and butter highest. Mine went against the ceiling, and, the butter being unusually thick, adhered.

I was in great alarm; there was no getting it down: it stuck, and neither the usher nor the master, when he entered for prayers, observed it.

During preparation of lessons, during prayers, my eyes reverted to the piece of bread and butter. It remained unnoticed. That it was also unobserved by the servants, who were supposed to clean the room, is not perhaps matter of surprise.

The next day passed—still the bread and butter hung suspended—but on the third day, during prayers, flop!—down it came in front of the master, and left behind it a nasty, greasy stain on the ceiling.

"Whose piece of bread and butter is that?" asked the master, when Amen had been said.

I had to confess, and was whipped.

That stain in the ceiling grew darker daily. The dust of the room adhered to the butter. It was not effaced all the while I remained a boarder, and I involuntarily every day, and frequently daily, looked at it, to see how much deeper the tinge was that the patch acquired.

Years after, when I was a man, and the old master was dead, and the house was in other hands, I ventured to ask the then tenants to be allowed to look at my old school-haunt. And—actually—the bread and butter stain was still there. Like murder—it could not be hid.

32

The ceiling had been repeatedly whitewashed, but ever through the coverings that overlaid it, the butter mark reasserted itself.

I cannot say whether it was this which causes me always, on entering a room, to direct my eyes to the ceiling—but I do, and observe it always with much interest.

The ceiling of the world is not one blank space; it is sprinkled with stars at night, and strewn with clouds by day. Why then should the ceilings of our rooms be blank surfaces? We spread carpets of colour on our floors. We decorate richly our walls. Why should the ceiling alone be left in hideous baldness, in fact, absolutely plain? White ceilings were a product of that worst period of art—savethe mark! that age of no art at all, the beginning of the present century.

The ceiling came in in the reign of Henry VIII., and reached its greatest perfection in that of Elizabeth. At a later period the ornamentation became richer, but not so tasteful.

The mouldings were worked with "putty lime," lime finely sifted and mixed with some hair, the lines of the ornamentation were made with ribbons of copper or lead, and the pattern was fashioned by hand over this.

It is supposed that the drops one finds in Tudor ceilings, and which are not of plaster, or plaster only, but of carved wood, are a mere ornament, and purposeless.

This, however, is not the case. Such enriched ceilings are very heavy, and their weight has a tendency to break down the laths to which they adhere, but these pendents are bolted into the rafters, and serve to form so many supports for the entire ceiling, which without them might in time fall.

The Elizabethan ceiling was geometrical in design, but with bands of flower-work, conventional in character, introduced, and sometimes consisted in strap-work, studded with rosettes, wondrously interlacing.

Then came a simpler geometrical pattern, circles enclosing wreaths of flowers copied from nature, exquisitely delicate and beautiful; but the imitation was carried sometimes too far, as when the flower heads are suspended on fine stalks of copper wire.

In a little squirarchical mansion in Cornwall, of no architectural beauty, there was a marvellously beautiful ceiling of the date of Charles II., the flowers and fruit infinitely varied, and wrought with exquisite delicacy. The room was low, and for that reason the artist had taken special pains in the modelling.

A "Brummagem" man bought up the land and the house—this latter was far too small to suit his ideas, and it was left unoccupied.

One day the rector said to him: "I want to have my school treat next Thursday—should rain fall, may I take the children into the old hall?"

"By all means," said the new squire; "but it will be stuffy: I will have it ventilated."

He at once went down with two carpenters and ripped strips through the lovely ceiling from one end of the room to the other, utterly destroying this incomparable work, that must have occupied the artist months of patient labour, and which had called forth the best efforts of his genius.

That is how mulish stupidity is every day destroying the achievements of genius. It is on a level with that of the chawbacon who, having got hold of a Stradella violin, broke it up to light his fire with the splinters.

There was, perhaps, a little heaviness in these ceilings—a little more than there ought to be, and the perfection of plaster work was attained in Germany at a somewhat later period, when the rococo ceilings came in. These were superb—not heavy, but rich with fancy and exquisite in delicacy. This never reached England, or if a foreign workman came here and did a ceiling or two, the art did not take root. Instead it died completely out, and we were left with quite plain ceilings or such as had a centre-piece, cast, of no style—vulgar, tasteless, and mechanical, and of plaster of Paris.

We have come now to recognize, tardily, the right of the ceiling to decoration, and are either papering it or covering it with lincrusta, or papier mâché, or asbestos "salamander" decoration, applied. This is better than nothing, but, of course, is mechanical and monotonous, and can never compete with the work that is the direct outcome of mental effort and manual dexterity.

In connection with a ceiling I subjoin the following story from a friend:

34

"In 1891 my head mason had an attack of influenza, and this fell on his nerves, and convinced that he had been ill-wished he consulted a white-witch at——, who informed him that he had been 'overlooked' by one of his own profession, and that he had applied too late for a cure to be effected. The man became terribly depressed; he wandered over the country, disappearing for days, and keeping his family in alarm, lest he should make away with himself.

"This went on for several years. He would do no work, he took no interest in anything, and could speak of nothing but his ailments. 'His heart was broke,' such was his description of himself. Well, I was about to rebuild a wing of my mansion, and to make of one large room a ball-room. I went to my bewitched mason and said to him, 'Thomas, I wish you would help me. I am very anxious to have a first-class decorated ceiling to that ball-room, and you know what these Londoners be: they do all by machinery, and you buy a ceiling by the yard—nasty, vulgar stuff I would be ashamed to have seen here. I'll tell you what it is, Thomas, those Londoners come out of town and sail about the country in the holiday time picking up ideas. I think we must show them how a thing in ceilings ought to be done, and let them understand that we are not such fools as they take us to be. Try your hand at my ball-room ceiling. Get it started at any rate.' The man was not a plasterer by profession, but he had done some plaster work for me, and took an interest in it.

"'Oh, sir!' said he, 'my heart is broke. I couldn't do it.'

"'What,' I answered, 'not to teach the Londoners a lesson?'

"'Well, I'll begin it, but never be able to finish it.'

"'Then begin it, man.'

"So he did. Between us we contrived to model roses and tulips, etc. And then we set to work casting and finishing off. Then came the glorious rainless summer of 1896. 'Thomas,' said I, 'we must get the walls of the ball-room up and roofed over before winter. Do now lend a hand with building. Then when bad weather comes on you can begin to set up the ceiling.' So all the summer he was building—did not miss a day, and this winter he is hard at work at his ceiling, full of interest and delight, and has recovered his good looks, and to a large extent forgotten his maladies, and by the time that the last rose is finished off, I trust he will be a sound man again."

Now what my friend wrote me conveys a moral. Our country

workmen, masons, carpenters, smiths, are not fools. They need only to be directed in the paths of good taste, to execute admirable work, as good as anything produced in former days. Do not over-teach and direct them, give them good examples, show them the principles of construction and decoration, and then, as much as may be, leave them to work the details out by themselves. They become intensely interested and proud of their work, and take all their friends and fellow-tradesmen to see it, whether it be in the church or the manor-house; and that this sort of education, producing results in the place, attaches them to their village home, goes without saying.

There was a grand old fellow, George Bevan by name, a mason, who worked in this parish when I was a boy. And now, whenever in alteration or in pulling down a bit of George Bevan's work is come upon, the masons stand still, shake their heads, and say, "As well blast a rock as put a pick into George Bevan's work." Then say I, "Aye, and a hundred years hence folk will say, 'This has been done by the White family. There were giants in those days.'"

Unhappily, many of our landed proprietors think it quite enough to build "neat" farmhouses and cottages, and pay no regard to beauty. It does not cost more to build what is beautiful than what is hideous; if they took pains to educate their local artisans to do work that is pleasing, they would be elevating them in culture, and, what is more, attaching them to those old homes of theirs that they have helped to make a delight to the eye; whereas, set them to build what is ugly, and even though ignorant of the principles of art, they are dimly conscious that the cottage they occupy is not a place pleasant to the eye, and not one they can ever grow to love.

CHAPTER VI

As the manor-house with its hall was the centre of the organization for civil purposes, so was the Church the religious centre of the parish. In a considerable number of cases it certainly occupies the place of the older temple, in which the thane or chief was godi or priest as well as law-man in his hall.

This was not always the case; a good many of our churches are of later and exclusively Christian foundation, and were then planted in such place as was determined by quite other considerations.

The parish church is full of interest connected with the parish, it has been built and decorated by the ancestors of the humble inhabitants of the place, the yard about it contains their dust; in it they have left something of their very best—to be swept away by the modern restorer to put in his own stuff, manufactured at a distance, the whole executed by a strange contractor employing strange workmen. The village people have done nothing towards it, but have looked on to see the monumental slabs of their forefathers torn up, some sawn in half and employed to line drains, the frescoes that their forbears had painted scraped away, the Jacobean altar rails turned by ancient carpenters of the village thrown forth to rot, and their place supplied by some painted and gilt stuff, procured from Messrs. This and That, near Covent Garden, chosen from an illustrated catalogue.

Some wiseacres cry out because antiquaries complain at this devastation, but have not these latter a right to complain when parochial history written in the parish church is being obliterated? And is it not better to leave things alone, than put them into the hands of strangers? In my own neighbourhood is a church, Bridestowe, that had a beautiful woodscreen. An incumbent gave up this church to a restorer. He cut down the screen, took the tracery of the screen-windows, sawed it in half, turned it upside down, and employed it to glue on to some wretched deal bench-ends, and to a breastwork screen to the chancel, and to ornament a deal door.

At Sheepstor was a gorgeous screen, rich with gold and colour. I remember it well. The church was delivered over to a local builder

37

to be made neat, and cheaply—above all, cheaply. He destroyed the entire screen, and left the church a horror to behold. Now the present rector has recovered a few poor fragments of the screen and has stuck them up, attached to a pillar with a box beneath, pleading for subscriptions for the reconstruction of what was wantonly destroyed fourteen years ago.

In the year 1851, when I was a boy of seventeen, I went a walking tour in Devonshire, and halted one day at Kenton to see the church. I found in it not only one of the finest screens in the county, but also the very finest carved oak pulpit, richly coloured and gilt. I at once made a careful working drawing of it to scale.

Years passed away, and not till 1882 did I revisit the church—when, judge my distress. It had been put into the hands of an architect to "restore," and he had restored the pulpit out of existence, and replaced it by the thing represented on the next page.

I at once asked the rector what had become of the old pulpit, which, by the way, had been hewn out of the trunk of an enormous oak tree. He replied that he knew nothing about it—except that he thought some scraps of the carving were in the National School. I then went to the school-house and questioned the master about it. He said that he believed there was some old carving in a cupboard— and there we found it, with dusters, old reading books, a dirty sponge, and any amount of cobwebs and filth. The rector kindly allowed me to carry away the scraps, and with them and my working drawing taken thirty-one years before we found that it was possible to reconstruct the old pulpit, and now—thanks to my cousin, who has illustrated this book, and the zeal of the new rector of Kenton—this splendid pulpit has been restored—really restored this time.

Let this be a lesson to rectors and others who put their poor churches into the hands of architects.

I do not know that human perversity is more conspicuous in anything than in the monstrous Belgian carved wooden pulpits, that are the admiration of visitors and the pride of sacristans. They are enormous erections of oak, marvellously pieced together, and carved to represent various sacred scenes, the figures being life-sized.

The pulpit in Antwerp Cathedral represents Europe, Asia, Africa, and America, in half-draped allegorical figures; above whose heads trees intertwine, with birds among the branches, and amidst leaves and beetles and lizards and snails appears the preacher as another lusus naturæ.

A good number of ancient pulpits remain in English churches, some of oak, others of stone. A pulpit of iron is said to have existed formerly in the Cathedral at Durham; and I have seen one such of very elaborate character at Feldkirchen, in the Vorarlberg.

Who can say but that we shall be having them in aluminium before long! There is a fashion in these things, and we are at the dawn of an aluminium age. That will have one advantage; it will see the close of the epoch of Bath-stone and marble pulpits, all ugly and unsuitable, in our cold northern climate, where the pulpit should be calculated to warm, not to chill.

There is a fashion not only in the material of which pulpits are made, but also in their structure. At one time they were very high up above the heads of the congregation, then they were let down very low, so that the preacher was scarce raised at all, and now they are pushed a little further up. In a church I know the central stem of the pulpit is of stout oak. When the fancy was that the preacher should be high up, then the end of the post was planted on the ground. Then came the fashion that it should be low, accordingly a deep hole was sunk with a pick under the base, and the post lowered into it. Presently it was considered that the lowness of the pulpit was too considerable, the preacher was inaudible at the end of the church; accordingly pick and spade were engaged again, and the post pulled half-height up again and there wedged. Here is a suggestion for future use. Why not have the stem telescopic? Then the whole body of the pulpit can be made to go up or come down, as suits the preacher's voice.

I remember some years ago hearing that Bishop Wilberforce when he ruled the See of Oxford was once, and once only, disconcerted in the pulpit. This was the occasion. He had gone to preach at the opening of a new church, or the restoration of an old one, I cannot recall which. Now one of the great improvements introduced was that the floor of the pulpit was so contrived as to work upon a screw to adapt the height within the pulpit to the occupant. The pulpit was circular internally, and as the screw turned it turned the floor round. The parish clerk was vastly pleased at the ingenuity and convenience of this arrangement, and considered that the reopening

39

of the church demanded imperatively the exhibition of the new mechanism. He waited till the bishop was in the pulpit, and had said, "Let us pray," when he went to the vestry and began to work the crank. To his inexpressible surprise Bishop Wilberforce found the book-board slipping from before his face, and that he was revolving, and facing in quite a different direction from that which he had taken up when he called for the prayers of the congregation.

Presently the red face of the clerk appeared looking approvingly through the vestry-door, to see how the mechanism worked, and then with renewed energy he fell to at the crank, and round went the prelate again, and his face to his great puzzlement was brought back to the book-board.

He got through the collect somehow, rose to his feet, and gave out the text.

To his infinite concern and perplexity he began his text facing the congregation, and ended it presenting his back to them. Not only so, but he was obviously rising out of his pulpit, or rising higher in it as he rotated on his axis.

It was in vain that he tried to begin his sermon, and shuffled into suitable position, the floor revolved under him, and the book-board and sides of the pulpit seemed to be sinking away from him. A sense of nausea, of sea-sickness, came over the right reverend father, and he feared that in another turn his knees would be level with the edge of the pulpit. He became giddy.

By this time the incumbent of the church had discovered what was in process, and precipitated himself into the vestry, threw himself on the crank, and worked it backwards with a vigour truly admirable, but with the result that he spun the bishop round in reverse order to that in which he had gone up, as he let him down to a suitable level.

As I heard the story, I learned that on this occasion the eloquence of Samuel Wilberforce deserted him.

How far the tale is true, I am not in a position to say. I tell the tale as it was current at the time.

A certain fluent pulpit orator, a great luminary in his theological school, had a spring contrivance at the back of his pulpit, into which he could throw himself, and in which he could sway his body from side to side.

The trumpet mouths in connection withtubes that are carried into pews occupied by deaf persons have given rise to mistakes.

One preacher, who was short-sighted, and who always harangued extempore, on entering the pulpit took off his spectacles, and, seeing something circular beside the desk, supposed it to be a shelf or bracket, and put the glasses on it, whereupon down shot the spectacles and blocked the tube. Another, who had been provided with a glass of water, emptied the vessel into the receiver, and the deaf old lady at the end of the tube received into her ear—not a gush of oratory, but a jet of water.

One hot summers day my wife and I happened to be at Eichstätt, in Bavaria; the day was Whitsun Eve. We tried the doors of a large church, and found them locked, with the exception of one small side door that opened out of a cloister, and we entered the church by that.

To my great surprise I heard a voice high pitched and ringing through the spacious vaults in earnest pastoral address. I thought this very odd, as no one was in the church save an old sacristan, who was dusting and decorating the side altars previous to the ceremonies of Whit-Sunday.

My wife and I strolled down the side aisle, looking at the pictures, and still the impassioned harangue pealed through the church. As we passed the sacristan he began to laugh. We went further, and, having seen all that was to be seen in the north aisle, emerged into the nave, with the purpose of crossing the church to look at the pictures in the south aisle, when we saw a young curé in the pulpit, gesticulating, pouring forth a fervid address to his dearly beloved brethren—who were conspicuously absent. Suddenly the preacher was aware of an English gentleman and lady as audience. He paused, lost the thread of his discourse, put his hand into his pocket for the MS., found it, but could not find his place; made a new rush at a sentence; his voice gave way, and, turning tail, he ran down the pulpit stairs, and darted out of the church in confusion. He was a young priest, recently ordained, practising his first sermon which he was to deliver on the morrow.

I have seen what is not often seen—women occupying a pulpit, and

41

that in a Roman Catholic church. It came about in this way. I was at Innsbrück when the marriage took place of the daughter of the Governor of Tyrol, Count Taaffe, with some distinguished nobleman.

The cathedral was crammed with all the élite of the place, and there was no seeing the blush on the cheek of the bride, for there was no seeing the bride at all for the crowd. Beside me were two very well-dressed ladies who were extremely troubled at this. I believe, however, they were more anxious to have a good sight of the bridegroom than of the bride.

"My dear Ottilie," whispered one to the other, "this will never do. I must, I positively must see them."

"But how, Nottburg, sweetest, is that to be done? We cannot get into the gallery, that is packed."

"My angel! packed or not packed, I simply must see the ceremony. I shall die if I don't."

"What can be done? There are women standing on the rails of the side altars."

"My Ottilie, it is a matter of life or death. I must see."

"But how?"

"Hold—the pulpit!"

Now the pulpit was a gorgeous affair of marble and gilding, and was accessible only by means of a little door in the wall. It was very high. At once Nottburg and Ottilie, clinging to each other, worked a way for themselves with their elbows, using them like fins, through the crowd towards this particular door. I watched them. No one else had thought of invading the pulpit. Through the door they went, and they bolted it behind them, and in another moment there they were, bonnets and feathers and smiles, in the pulpit, and no one could dislodge them, as they had secured the door behind.

I have said there is a fashion in pulpits, and there is caprice as well. A very eloquent preacher I know entertains the idea of having space in which to stride about. Accordingly he set up in his new church an oblong platform, measuring 10 ft. by 5 ft., and he enclosed it with a plain deal railing, 3 ft. 6 in. high. He himself being a very tall man, this suited him admirably. He would place both his hands on the rail, and swing the upper portion of his body over when he sought to be impressive. Unhappily, for a great festival, he invited by letter a stranger, whom he had never seen, to preach for him. On the arrival of the strange preacher, he proved to be a very small man indeed. Still, I do not think it occurred to the incumbent to make provision, nor did he realize what the result would be, till the Preacher of the Day ascended the pulpit, when, at once, by rector, by choir, by the entire congregation, it was seen that the sermon could, would, must be nothing but a farce. The preacher was visible in the pulpit—and looked for all the world like a white rabbit hopping about in a cage, his head could hardly be seen over the top.

At once vergers were sent with hassocks, and two of these were placed in the pulpit, one balanced on top of the other, and on this the little man had to maintain his equilibrium—or seek to maintain it, not always successfully, as at intervals one hassock would slip away, whereupon the preacher's head disappeared, and the sermon was interrupted while he chased the evading hassock and replaced it as a footstool.

When I was an undergraduate at Cambridge there was a very little man incumbent of a certain church, and not only was he little, but there was something indescribably comical in his appearance. The only occasion on which I went to service there this odd little man mounted the pulpit with great solemnity and gave out as his text: "I am fearfully and wonderfully made." I can remember nothing of his sermon, but the sight of the droll little object in the pulpit giving out this text is ineffaceable in my memory.

There is one feature of the ancient pulpit which is not now reproduced. This is the sounding-board. No sounding-boards were employed to assist the voice in mediæval churches, but then such churches were built in proportions acoustically suitable, and it is hard to find an ancient church in which the voice does not travel easily. The forming of square and high pews no doubt did much to interfere with ease in preaching, as every such pew became a trap for catching the waves of sound. Consequently the device of a sounding-board was introduced when churches were chopped up into boxes, and the voice needed concentration and assistance. When the pews disappeared, the need for the sounding-board ceased and it has disappeared likewise.

In one of the groups of islands in the South Pacific where the

43

Wesleyan missionaries have succeeded in converting the natives, a friend of mine was desirous of doing something as a recognition of much kindness which he had received from the chief, and before leaving the island he asked the chief what he could let him have as a token of his regard. The native replied that there was one thing he and his people craved for with all the ardour of their fiery tropical blood—and this was a pulpit. In the island of Rumtifoo visible in the offing, the converts had a very fine pulpit in their chapel, but here in this island was none; would Mr. X—— give him a pulpit? The Englishman pondered. He had never in his life made a pulpit, and he had never accurately observed the organic structure of a pulpit, so as to know how to set about to make one. However, in his desire to oblige, he took counsel with an English sailor, and these two set to work to design and execute a pulpit.

Their initial difficulty was, however, how to get the proper material. No wood boards were to be had except some old champagne cases. These cases were knocked to pieces, and out of the boards an octagonal pulpit was reared.

When got into shape the two Englishmen walked round it, eyed it, and agreed that something was wanting to complete it, and that was a book-desk. Accordingly this was fashioned out of some more pieces of the champagne cases and fastened to the pulpit, which was now removed to the chapel and set in position.

The English makers of the pulpit next seated themselves in front of it and studied with a critical and, as far as possible, an impartial eye. Both agreed that it would not quite do as it was, for on the boards composing the sides were drawn in black large champagne bottles, and there were fragments of the inscription, "This side up," worked into the structure.

"It must be painted," said my friend.

"It must—certainly," responded the sailor. "It don't look quite as it ort."

But no paint was procurable in the island. However, it was discovered that a pot of Aspinall's enamel was in the island of Rumtifoo, and the chief managed to negotiate an exchange—whether an ox, or so many cocoanuts, or a wife was given for the enamel pot I cannot remember.

The pot, when procured, proved to be one of emerald-green. The brighter the better, thought my friend; and he and the sailor proceeded to paint the pulpit, and cover over the inscription and the bottles.

Great was the eagerness of the native chief to have the pulpit opened, and he sent to the island of Kokabundi for a native evangelist to occupy the pulpit for the first time, and sanctify it.

The evangelist came. The chapel was crammed with native Christians, and the preacher ascended the emerald-green pulpit.

All went well for a while, all went very well till the preacher warmed to his subject, and then he laid hold of the book-desk and swung himself about, and banged on it with his sable fists, till—crack, smash!—the book-desk went to pieces.

Nothing disconcerted, rather roused to more vehement action and harangue, the evangelist now laid hold of the sides of the pulpit, he dashed himself from side to side, he almost precipitated himself over the edge, he grappled with the flanks, and pulled this way, that way, till—crack! smash!—the sides began to gape like a tulip that is going off bloom, and presently away went one side, then another, and the whole pulpit was a wreck.

But this was not all; the paint had not been given time thoroughly to dry; the hands of the orator were moist, not to say sticky, and the paint came off on his fingers and palms, and as he wiped his face, dripping with perspiration, he left on it great smearsof emerald enamel on nose and eyebrows, cheek and chin.

The congregation was worked up as by a magnetic influence: it sighed, allelujahed, groaned, swayed, the women laid hold of each others tresses and pulled as they rocked themselves, and when the preacher banged on the desk, the native males in sympathy banged on each other's pates as well. Some screamed, some fell on their backs and kicked. Indeed, never since the conversion of the island had there been known such a rousing revival as on this occasion; and great was the exultation of the natives to think that one of their own preachers by his fervour had "busted up" an English-made pulpit.

And now a few words on the old gallery at the west end of the church, at present disappearing everywhere.

In every man's life there have been mistakes upon which he looks

45

back with self-reproach. Such a mistake was that which I made on entering on the incumbency of East Mersea, in Essex.

A deputation waited on me, consisting of labourers, who asked that I would restore the old instrumental music in the church, which had been abolished by my predecessor.

Now my predecessor had provided a costly harmonium, of the best procurable quality. I had to consider this. I considered, moreover, the agonies I had endured as a boy from the performance of a west gallery orchestra; so I declined to entertain the project.

Next Sunday was windy. There was in the church a stove, and to the stove-pipe outside a cowl. In the wind the cowl twisted and groaned. Afterwards I learned from a superior farmer's wife, that, having heard of the purpose of the deputation to call on me, at the first groan of the cowl her blood ran cold; with horror in all her nerves she thought—"He has given way. Here is the orchestra tuning up!"

I regret, however, that I did not yield, for I believe now that no old institution should be abolished that is capable of improvement. It is quite true that the performances were torturing to the ear that was educated, nevertheless they were the best that the village musicians could produce, and therefore ought not to have been rejected. There was in them an element of life, they were capable of improvement, and they were homegrown.

The harmonium was a new instrument, it had to be played by the schoolmistress, an importation; and, after all, a harmonium is an odious instrument, only a degree better than the old village orchestra.

But I think that it was not merely the painfulness of the performances of the old orchestra that caused their abolition. I am sure that many a parson would have gone on enduring, having his ears tortured and his teeth set on edge, had it not been for the discords in the instrumentalists, as well as in the instruments.

The quarrels in the west gallery were proverbial. Strikes had begun there long before they began in factories and coal-mines. Sometimes the strikes were against the parson, if he interfered with the orchestra for intemperate proceedings—leaving bottles of ale and spirits, or rather leaving bottles that had contained these liquors—in the gallery after practice night. Sometimes the strikes were against the conductor, or the first violin, and I have a recollection of one of the strikes being an emphatic one, when the fiddle-stick performed its part on the head of the flute, and the flute on the head of the fiddle.

There was a dear old rector I remember, who said once: "I never can be brought to believe that there will be music in heaven, for if there be music there, there must be choirs and orchestra; and if choirs and orchestra, then there can be no harmony."

The bickerings, the heart-burnings, in the west gallery were a constant source of trouble to the parson, and if he seized on a means of establishing peace by abolishing the orchestra, he was not altogether to blame.

The first stage in getting rid of the village orchestra was taken by the introduction of the barrel-organ. I can well recall that stage.

Now the barrel-organ had but a limited range of tunes. Our organ had a vein of lightness and wantonness in it. How this came about I do not know. But one of the tunes ground out on it was "The Devil's Hop." This would never do. There were two elements of difficulty in it. In the first place, if this tune were not turned on we would be one tune the poorer in divine service. But it was intolerable that any psalm should be sung to "The Devil's Hop." After much consideration the difficulty was solved in this way. On the organ the title "The Devil's Hop" was altered into "De Ville's Hope," and instructions were issued to the grinder to grind slowly and solemnly. By this means the air served for an Easter psalm.

I possess a very interesting manuscript. A great-uncle of mine, the late Sir Edward Sabine, when a youth, was on one of the early Polar expeditions. Whilst he was absent, a cousin kept a diary of the daily doings at home, for his entertainment on his return. This was in 1819. I believe my great-uncle never read the MS., but I have done so with great delight.

Now in it occurs this entry:

"To-day—walked to South Mimms Church where a novelty has been introduced—a barrel-organ in the west gallery, in place of the old orchestra. I listened and thought it very beautiful, but I do not approve of these changes in divine service. To what will they lead? Where will be the end?"

My dear relative who penned these words is long since dead. What would she have said had she lived to the present day?

The barrel-organ is gone now. It is a thing of the past. The next stage was a little wheezing organ that cost about £20, sometimes even less. Horrible little things they were, broken-winded, giving out squeaks and puffs, and with no bass notes at all. Moreover, they were always getting out of order.

One had been introduced into a neighbouring church in place of the discarded barrel-organ, and the neighbourhood was invited to be present on the Sunday in which it was to be "opened." But alas! It had opened itself in an unexpected and irremediable manner—irremediable on the spur of the moment, and by inexperienced persons. There had been damp weather, and the leather of the bellows had become unglued.

The blower bowed to his work when the organ voluntary was to begin. "Hussh-h-h!" a puff. The keys were struck, with more vigour the blower laboured, and louder sounded the puffs—and nothing was heard save the puffs. Then the clerk left his desk and went to the gallery to open an inquiry. Presently, after much whispering and knocking about of seats in the gallery, the clerk came to the front, with a red face, and announced ore rotundo, "This here be to give notice. This here dratted orging ain't going to play this here Sunday. 'Cos hers busted her belleys."

When there had been a fracas among the instrumentalists, or when the organ had "busted," then the choir had to sustain the burden of the singing unsupported. And sometimes when the organ or organist was unequal to some new anthem on a high festival, the choir had to perform by itself.

I recollect one notable occasion. It was Christmas. The village choir was intent on performing the Hallelujah Chorus from the "Messiah." Bless you, my dear readers! they were not timorous and hesitating in those days any more than in these, when only quite recently a young village carpenter proposed for a rustic parish entertainment a piece out of "Lohengrin."

To return to the Hallelujah Chorus. Unhappily the organist was bowled over by a severe cold and could not attend. The soprano was cook at the rectory, and the plum-pudding had somehow gone wrong and must be attended to. So she did not attend. The alto had been invited "with her young man" to a friend's at a distance, therefore she could not attend, and the bass had been out carolling all night and drinking ale, and was hoarse and—well, indisposed. Accordingly, nothing daunted, our tenor gave us the Hallelujah Chorus as a solo, without accompaniment at all, and without the other parts. That was a wonderful performance—never to be forgotten.

The other day I was in a restored church, with stained glass windows, with brass candelabra, with velvet and gold hangings, with carved oak bench-ends, and encaustic tiled floors, and—I could not help myself—I laughed; for I saw in the side chapel a huge organ, elaborately painted and gilt. It had three key-boards, and I could not count all the stops. Nothing to laugh at in that; no: but there was, in the contrast between the church as it is now and what it was fifty years ago, as I remember it. I was then in it on a Sunday. There were no carved benches then, but tall deal pews. There was no organ: there was an orchestra in the west gallery, and the clerk was first violin therein. But his duties required that he should sit near the reading-desk at the chancel arch. Now, when it came to the giving out a psalm, the old fellow stood up and announced: "Let us sing to the praise and glory of God the—— Psalm." Having done this, he left his desk and strode down the nave whistling the tune very shrilly, till he reached the west gallery, where he took his place at the music-stand, and drew the bow across his fiddle, tuned it, and the whole orchestra broke out into music—or, to be more exact, uproar.

In small country parishes it was by no means infrequent that the clerk alone could read, and he had to do all the responses. When it came to the psalm, he read out two lines audibly. Whereupon choir and congregation sang those two lines. Then he gave out two more lines, and those were sung. So on to the end. This was not very musical; but what else could be done, when the power to read print was not present in the congregation?

I do not think that the true history of the west end gallery in a parish church is properly known. In mediæval churches there was a very rich and elaborately carved wood screen between the chancel and the body of the church. The screen had several purposes to serve, some symbolical, some liturgical, some practical.

In the first place it was symbolical of death. In the Tabernacle and Temple a veil hid the Holy of Holies; but on the death of Christ the

49

veil was rent asunder from the top to the bottom, and this signified that the way into the Holiest Place was open to all, and that death ceased to be the impenetrable mysteryit had been; since Christ, by His death, had overcome death, it was possible to look beyond the veil and see the glorious place where is the Mercy-Seat and the Altar-Throne, and where our Great High Priest standeth, ever making intercession for us.

Now, in the mediæval churches, the chancel represented the Holiest Place, or heaven, and the nave was the figure of the Church on earth. Consequently the screen, dividing the nave from the chancel, was a figure of death. But inasmuch as by faith we can look through and beyond the barrier of death, the screens were made of carved work pierced through, so that the chancel with the altar might be perfectly visible beyond the screen. And inasmuch as death was overcome by Christ, the crucifix stood above the screen, a figure that proclaimed that it was through the cross of Christ alone, that the kingdom of heaven was opened to all believers, and that death was swallowed up in victory.

So much for the symbolic meaning of the screen. And yet, no—one word more must be added. Last summer I was walking along the north coast of Devon, when I visited the very fine parish church of Coombe Martyn. This noble church possesses an exceedingly fine rood-screen that has not been demolished. The church possesses something else of interest—a very intelligent, quaint old parish clerk.

As I was admiring the screen, the old man, who was dusting in the church, came up to me and said: "Please, your honour, have y' ever heard tell why the screen-doors niver shut?"

I expressed my doubt that this was so.

"Now, do y' go and look at ivery old church screen you seez," said the clerk. "If it ho'n't been meddled wi' by them blessed restorers, you'll find for sure sartain that the oak doors won't shut. Zur, see here. Here be the doors. Try 'em; they can't be made to shut."

I answered that the wood had swelled, and the joinery was imperfect.

"No, your honour," said the old man. "If you look close, you'll see it was made on purpose not to fit."

50

On examination it certainly did appear that the doors in question never could have been fastened. I admitted this, but doubted whether it was the same with all screen-gates.

"It's the same wi' all," said the old man. "I've looked at scores, and they was all made just the same, on purpose not to fit."

"That is very odd," said I, still incredulous.

"It was done on purpose," said the old man.

Then he came out with his explanation.

"Doant y' see, your honour. Them old men as made the screens weren't bad joiners, and they weren't fules neither. They was a sight better joiners than we be now. The reason they did it was this. For sure sartain the chancel means heaven, and the body of the church means airth. And then, doan't it say in Scriptur, 'The gates shall not be shut at all?' Very well, if the chancel be meant to tell o' the heavenly Jerusalem, then the screen gates must be made not to fit, that never nobody may never be able to fasten 'em no more. The old men weren't bad joiners, nor fules—not they."

And now—to the liturgical significance of the screen. As already said, it supported the crucifix, and the rule was that during Lent all images were to be veiled or covered with wraps. Accordingly, on the top of the screens were galleries by means of which the crucifix could be reached for the veiling on Shrove Tuesday, and the unveiling on Easter Eve.

But the screen served a third purpose, and that was eminently practical. On it sat the orchestra and choir. The gallery was made broad and solid to support them, and was furnished with a back to the west, against which the performers might lean, and which concealed them from the congregation in the nave. These backs have for the most part disappeared; nevertheless, several remain. They naturally were the first part of a screen to give way through the pressure of somnolent human beings against it.

The choir and instrumentalists sat on the rood-screen, where they could see every movement of the priest at the altar, and so take their cues for singing and playing. It was essential that they should be in this position. In Continental churches, where in many places the screens have been mutilated or removed, the choirs still occupy

51

their old places. For instance, at Bruges, where the screen in the cathedral is reduced to a mere block of black and white marble beside the chancel steps, the musicians remain perched at the top. At Freiburg, where the screen and gallery have been erected in one of the transepts, quite out of sight of the altar, the singers and orchestra are on it.

At the Reformation, when the crucifix was torn away, a great ugly gap was left in the gallery-back above the screen. In cathedrals this gap was filled up with the organ. And in cathedrals and large churches the organ displaced the instrumentalists.

In many churches the screen itself was destroyed or allowed to fall into decay. But the use of the gallery was not forgotten. The priest now occupied the reading-desk, and as this was very generally in the body of the church, something had to be done to bring the choir and orchestra into a suitable position facing him.

Accordingly, in a great number of cases the gallery was removed to the west end of the church, and those who rendered the musical portion of divine service moved with it. Hence it came about that in a vast majority of cases the gallery at the west end, under the tower arch, came to be the great focus and centre of music and discord.

Now the fashion has set in everywhere to pull down the west gallery and open out the tower arch. But when the west gallery is gone, whither is the organ to go? Where is the choir to be put? The choirs are now very generally accommodated in the chancel, but the organ has been moved about into various places more or less unsuitable.

At one time the fashion was to build out a sort of chapel on the north side and to fit the organ into it; boxing it up on all sides but one. Naturally, the organ objected to this treatment. It was made to occupy an open space: it demanded circulation of air. In the pocket into which it was thrust it became damp, and went out of tune.

Nothing could have been designed more senseless than these cramped chapels for organs. The organ sets waves of air in motion, and the walls boxing in the pipes prevented the waves from flowing. It was found that organs in this position did not give forth a volume of sound commensurate with their cost and size, and they were pulled out, and stuck in side aisles, and painted and gilt, and an attempt made to render an unsightly object comely by flourish of decoration.

But again difficulties and objections became evident. An organ ought not to be on the damp floor, and it ought to be well elevated. Moreover, planted at the east end of an aisle, it did not support the congregation in their singing. It roared and boomed in the ears of the choir; and if the service is to be an elaborate performance, in which the congregation takes the part of audience only, then it is in the right place. But if the divine worship is to be congregational, if all are to be encouraged to sing, then the organ is out of place.

Consequently in a good many cases there is a talk of moving back the organ into a west gallery.

Unhappily, an organ is a very expensive traveller. An individual can tour round the globe at about the same cost that will move an organ from one end of a church to another. Hundreds on hundreds of pounds have been spent in marching the unhappy organ about; and we cannot be sure that its wanderings are over yet.

In these restless and impatient days, when everyone has a theory and a scheme, and desires to do what is contrary to what has been done, the hardest of lessons to acquire, and that entailing most self-restraint, but that which is least costly, and most calculated to give a man peace at the last, is to let well alone.

And now before we leave the old church, something must be said about the tower and bells.

On the Continent there is absolutely no art in bell-ringing—it is what any fool can do; the bells are clashed together, there is no sequence of notes, no changes in succession, there is noise, not melody. I remember many years ago passing through the queer little village with a queerer name, Corpsnuds, in theFrench Landes, on Midsummer-day. From the quaint church-tower sounded the most extraordinary clatter of bells, without sequence and without harmony. Moreover, from the top of the tower fluttered an equally extraordinary flag. On more attentive examination of the latter, when the wind was sufficiently strong to unfurl and expand it, it became obvious that this flag was nothing more nor less than a pair of dingy black trousers split at the seam, and reseated with a dingy navy-blue patch.

Having made the observation, I entered the belfry, to ascertain what produced the clatter among the bells.

There I discovered the sexton, in his blouse, very hot, very red, profusely perspiring, racing about the interior swinging the end of a single bell-rope.

On seeing me he halted, and wiped his brow on his sleeve. I asked him how it was that he alone was able to ring a peal of bells.

"Mais!" he answered, "C'est bien possible. I have tied a broomstick in a knot of the rope, among the bells, and as I whisk the rope about, the stick rattles this bell, that bell, all of them. Voila tout!"

"And the banner waving augustly above the tower?" I further inquired.

"Bien simple," was his answer. "An old pair of my patched pantaloons. My wife slit them; we have no parish flag, so I said— allons! mes pantalons. There they are: aloft! One must do what one can in honour of the bon Saint Jean."

It is in England alone that bell-ringing is an art, and oh! how lovely an art it is—to those far away who hear the swell and fall of the bells, the music always having a certain sadness in it. But it has its sordid side, as has all art, and the sordid side is the interior of the belfry; or, let us say, was, before reform pushed its way there.

There was some excuse for the ringers to conduct themselves in a free and easy manner in the belfry when it was shut off from the body of the church by a screen of boards against which the west gallery was erected. Then the belfry was so much apart from the church that it ceased to be regarded as pertaining to it, or being included within its sacred atmosphere. Accordingly the ringers conducted themselves in the belfry as they saw fit. They introduced pipes, also a barrel of beer. They sketched each other on the boards, never in complimentary style. They wrote scurrilous verses on the screen, and sometimes conducted there all kinds of buffoon games, and played practical jokes on each other.

Not only did they consider that they might do as they liked in the belfry, but that they might have access to it when they liked, and ring on whatever occasion they pleased.

Another abuse crept in. The ringers considered that they had done quite sufficient when they had rung a peal before Divine Service. Their ringing ended, they would withdraw to the road or loiter about the churchyard, talking and smoking, whilst worship proceeded within the church.

54

In a certain place that I know the ringers had been allowed their own way under an indifferent rector, and the worst possible condition of affairs had resulted. Then came a new rector with the reforming spirit in him, and he resolved to put matters to right. Hitherto the belfry key had been retained by the sexton, a prime offender. The parson demanded it. The sexton refused to surrender it. Then the rector went with a blacksmith to the tower door, broke it open, and affixed a new lock to it with a key that he retained for himself.

Great was the indignation among the ringers, and an anonymous letter was received by the rector:

"This be to giv Nottis. If you pass'n doant mind wot your about and let we ring the bells as plazes we, then us wull knock your little 'ed off."

The rector was not to be intimidated. That night he went to the belfry and locked himself in.

At the usual time for the practice to begin the ringers arrived, and he heard them discuss him and his doings in the churchyard. That he did not mind.

"I say," remarked the sexton, "ain't he the minister? Wot do that mean but that he's sent by the bishop to minister to us and do jist as us likes?"

"Shure, b'aint no meanin' in words if that ain't it," responded another.

"Us won't be pass'n-ridden," said a third.

"Us'll break open the door," said a fourth.

"And if he interferes, us'll scatt his little head open," said a fifth, "as us wrote he—you knaws."

Then came a bang against the tower door.

Now there happened to be a little window close to the door, just large enough for a man to put his head, but not his shoulders, through.

"I put on the lock, and I'll have it off," said the blacksmith. "I've brought a bar o' iron on purpose."

55

Then the rector put his head through the window, and said, "Will you? Here's my little head, scatt that first."

The men drew back disconcerted.

He had gained the day, and established his authority over the ringers, and control of the belfry door.

And now, in the same place, there is as well-conducted a set of ringers as may be found anywhere, and some of the old lot are still there. The first step in the reform of the belfry was that of obtaining mastery over the key.

A second step was taken when the west gallery was demolished and the tower-arch thrown open, so that the bell-ringers were visibly in the church, and so came to feel that they were in a sacred building in which there must be no profanity.

In several instances much good has been done by the rector or the curate becoming himself a ringer, or, if not that, taking a lively interest in the ringing, and being present in the belfry, or visiting it, on practising nights.

Some curious customs remain connected with bell-ringing. In Yorkshire it is customary when there occurs a death in the parish to toll the bell. Three strokes thrice repeated signify an adult male; three strokes twice repeated signify an adult female; two, two, three, a male infant; two, two, two, a female child. These strokes are then followed by as many as there were years in the age of the deceased. At Dewsbury and at Horbury, near Wakefield, on Christmas Eve, at midnight, the devils knell is rung. When I was curate at the latter place, at first I knew nothing of this singular knell. On my first Christmas Eve I had retired to bed, when at midnight I heard the bell toll.

Now, my window looked out into the churchyard, and was, in fact, opposite the tower door. I was greatly shocked and distressed, for I had not heard that anyone was ill in the parish, and I feared that the deceased must have passed away without the ministrations of religion.

I threw up my window and leaned out, awaiting the sexton. I counted the strokes—three, three, three: then I counted the ensuing strokes up to one hundred.

Still more astonished, I waited impatiently the appearance of the sexton.

When he issued from the tower, I called to him:

"Joe, who is dead?"

The man sniggered and answered, "T'owd un, they say."

"But who is dead?"

"T'owd chap."

"What old man? He must be very old indeed."

"Ay! he be owd; but for sure he'll give trouble yet."

It was not till next day that my vicar explained the matter to me.

At Dewsbury the devil's knell is thus accounted for. A certain bell there, called Black Tom of Sothill, is said to have been an expiatory gift for a murder, and the tolling is in commemoration of the execution of the murderer. One Thomas Nash, in 1813, bequeathed £50 a year to the ringers of the Abbey Church, Bath, "on condition of their ringing on the whole peal of bells, with clappers muffled, various solemn and doleful changes on the 14th of May in every year, being the anniversary of my wedding-day; and also on the anniversary of my decease, to ring a grand bob-major and merry peals unmuffled, in joyful commemoration of my happy release from domestic tyranny and wretchedness."

A singular and beautiful custom still subsists in the village of Horningsham, Wilts, where, at the burial of a young maiden, "wedding peals" are rung on muffled bells.

At the induction of a new vicar or rector it is customary for him to lock himself into the church, and then proceed to the belfry and "ring himself in." It is, I believe, universal in England for the parishioners to count the number of strokes he gives, as these are said to indicate the number of years during which he will hold the cure.

There still remain in some places certain forcible evidences that the ringers regaled themselves in the belfries, and these have taken the shape of ale-jugs. At Hadleigh, in Suffolk, is such a pitcher of brown glazed earthenware, that holds sixteen quarts, and bears this inscription:

> "We, Thomas Windle, Isaac Bunn, John Mann, Adam Sage, George Bond, Thomas Goldsborough, Robert Smith, Harry West."

and below the names are these lines:

> "If you love me doe not lend me,
> Use me often and keep me cleanly,
> Fill me full, or not at all,
> If it be strong, and not with small."

At Hinderclay, a ringer's pitcher is still preserved in the church tower, with the inscription on it:

> "From London I was sent,
> As plainly doth appear:
> It was with this intent,
> To be filled with strong beer.
> Pray remember the pitchers when empty."

In a closet of the steeple of St. Peters, Mancroft, Norwich, is another, that holds thirty-five pints. At Clare is a similar jug that holds over seventeen quarts, and one at Beccles that will contain six gallons less one pint.

As already said, the church bells, which the ringers regarded as their own, or as parish property, they chose to ring on the most unsuitable occasions, as when a "long main" at cock-fighting had been won. Church bells were occasionally rung for successful racehorses. In the accounts of St. Edmund's, Salisbury, is this entry:

> "1646. Ringing the race-day, that the Earl of Pembroke his horse winne the cuppe—— v$^{sh.}$"

At Derby, when the London coach drove through the town in olden times it was usual to announce its arrival by ringing the church bells, that all such as had fish coming might hasten to the coach and secure the fish whilst fairly fresh.

It used to be said that St. Peter's six bells, which first sounded the approach of the London coach, called "Here's fresh fish come to town. Here's fresh fish come to town." Next came All Saints', further

58

up the street, with its peal of ten, "Here's fine fresh fish just come into the town. Here's fine fresh fish just come into the town." Close by All Saints' stood St. Michael's, with but three bells, and one of them cracked, and the strain of this peal was, "They're stinking; they're stinking!" But St. Alkmund replied with his six, a little further on in the street, "Put more salt on 'em, then. Put more salt on 'em, then."

The earliest bells we have are the Celtic bells of hammered bronze, in shape like sheep bells, and riveted on one side. When these bells were first introduced they caused great astonishment, and many stories grew up about them. Thus, in the church of Kelly, in Devon, is an old stained-glass window that represents St. Oudoc, Bishop of Llandaff, with a golden yellow bell at his side. The story is told of him that he was one day thirsty, and passing some women who were washing clothes, he asked of them a draught of water. They answered laughingly that they had no vessel from which he could drink. Then he took a pat of butter, and moulded it into the shape of a cup or bell, and filled it with water, and drank out of it. And this golden bell remained in the church of Llandaff till it was melted up by the commissioners of Henry VIII.

A still more wonderful story was related of St. Keneth, of Gower, who, as a babe, was exposed in an osier coracle to the waves. The seagulls fluttered over him, and bore him to a ledge of rock, where they made a bed for him of the feathers from their breasts. Then they brought him a brazen bell to serve as baby's bottle, and every day the bell was filled with milk by a forest doe.

It is with bells as with all the faculties of man. They are all "very good" when used harmoniously; but the "sweet bells" can be "jangled out of tune" not only by the failure of mental power—as in the case of Hamlet—but by lack of balance and order in the moral sense.

CHAPTER VII

"I will take mine ease at mine inn!"

What an element of coziness, hospitality, picturesqueness is introduced into the village by the inn! There is another side—but that we will not consider.

I know some villages from which the squire has banished the hostelry, and poor, forlorn, half-hearted places they seem to me. If there be a side to the village inn that is undesirable, I venture to think that the advantage of having one surpasses the disadvantages. What the squire has done in closing the inn he hardly realizes. He has broken a tradition that is very ancient. He has snapped a tie with the past. In relation to quite another matter, Professor G. T. Stokes says: "History is all continuous. Just as the skilful geologist or palæontologist can reconstruct from an inspection of the strata of a quarry the animal and vegetable life of past ages, so can the historian reconstruct out of modern forms, rites, and ceremonies, often now but very shadowy and unreal, the essential and vigorous life of society as it existed ten centuries ago. History, I repeat, is continuous. The life of societies, of nations, and of churches is continuous, so that the life of the present, if rightly handled, must reveal to us much of the life of the past."[5] So is it with the parish; and so the dear old village inn has its story of connection with the manor, and its reason for being, in remote antiquity.

I have gone to Iceland to illustrate the origin of the manor, I shall go to Tyrol to explain the beginnings of the village inn—that is to say the manorial inn with its heraldic sign, in contradistinction to the church house, with its ecclesiastical sign. Each has its history—and each derives from a separate institution.

What is the origin of signs? The earliest signs were certainly heraldic. We have still in many villages the "So-and-so Arms," with the shield of the lord of the manor emblazoned upon it with all its quarterings. Or we have the Red Lion, or the White Hart, or the Swan, all either crests or cognizances of a family, or of a sovereign

---

[5] reland and the Celtic Church, London, 1892, p. 276.

or queen. The Swan sign is said to date from Anne of Cleves; the White Hart was the badge of Richard II., and inns with this sign probably were erected in that reign, and have retained this cognizance unchanged since. We know of inns under the name of the Rose, which there can be little question came into life as hostelries in the time of the Yorkists and Lancastrians. The Wheatsheaf was the Burleigh badge, the Elephant that of Beaumont, the Bull's Head was a Boleyn cognizance, the Blue Boar the badge of the De Veres, Earls of Oxford; the Green Dragon of the Earls of Pembroke, the Falcon of the Marquis of Winchester.

It does not, however, follow that the inns that have these signs date from the periods when, let us say, Anne Boleyn was queen, because they bear the token of the Bull's Head, or from the reign of Queen Elizabeth, when Burleigh was in power, because of the Wheatsheaf; for it will not infrequently be found that they take their titles and signs from a much more local origin, the coat or cognizance of the squire who holds the manor.

There was a reason for this: the inn was originally the place where the true landlord, i.e. the lord of the land, received his guests, and every traveller was his guest. In Iceland at the present day there is but one inn at Reykjavik, the capital, and that is kept by a Dane. The traveller in the island goes to any farmhouse or parsonage, and is taken in. Indeed, by law a traveller cannot be refused hospitality. When he leaves he makes a present either of money or of something else that will be valued, but this is a present, and not a payment. In many parts of Tyrol it is much the same. The excursionist is put up at the priest's house. The writer has been thus received, among other places, at Heiligkreutz, in the Oetz Thal. In the evening the room—the curé's parlour—was filled with peasants who asked for wine, and were supplied. When they left they put money in the hand of the pastor's sister, whilst he, smoking his pipe, looked out of the window. When the writer left next morning the same farce was enacted. Further up the same valley is Vent, where again the curé receives travellers, and his sister receives the payment, but there a definite charge is made; but at Heiligkreutz what was given was accepted as a present. The priests who entertain do not of course hang up signs over their doors. The pastor is supposed to be given to hospitality, and would give of his all freely and cheerfully if he could afford it; but of late years, as travellers have become more numerous, his pittance has become smaller, so that his hospitality can no longer be gratuitous.

61

In the old romances of chivalry we read of travellers always seeking the castle of someknight, and asking, almost demanding, lodging and entertainment.

Hospitality was a duty among the Germanic races. According to Burgundian law, the Roman who received a traveller was not allowed to do so gratis; the poorer Burgundian host was bound to pay the Roman for the keep of the traveller if he was unable to accommodate him in his own house. The honour of receiving a guest freely was too great to be conceded to a conquered people. When Theodoric with his Ostrogoths conquered Italy they were amazed at the Roman tavern system, and at the iniquity of the taverners, who had double measures, a just one for natives and an unjust one for foreigners. Why, the traveller should be treated freely, the Ostrogoth argued; and Cassiodorus, under the orders of the king, drew up laws to enforce at least honesty, if he could not bring about liberality, in the Latin osteria. We are inclined to be overhard in our judgment of the knights and barons of Germany in the Middle Ages, whose castles are perched on every commanding rock by every road and river, but we are scarcely just. It is true that there were robber knights, but so there are at all times rascals among a class, and we are wrong in supposing that every ruined keep was the nest of a robber knight. It was not so. The knights kept the roads in order, and supplied mules and horses to travellers; they also gave them free hospitality when they halted for the night. The travellers paid a small toll for the maintenance of the road, and also for the use of the horses and mules which carried them on to the next stage. On the navigable rivers the barons kept the tow-path and supplied the beasts which would drag the barges up the stream, and for this also they received, and very properly, a toll.

Here and there an ill-conditioned knight exacted more than was his due, but he was speedily reduced to order. It was to the interest of all the knights and barons along the highway to keep the communication open, and not to divert it into another channel; consequently when one member of the confraternity was exacting and troublesome the rest combined against him, or his over-lord reduced him to reason.

As the knights and barons had their castles on heights for purposes of defence, and these heights were considerable, it was not convenient for the wayfarers at the end of a toilsome journey to have to scramble up the side of a mountain to the castle of the lord to enjoy his hospitality. Accordingly they were entertained by him below in the village built on the highway. Moreover, he himself did not always inhabit the castle. It was irksome to him, and his wife and servants, to be perched on a rock like an eagle, consequently in time of peace he lived in his "town house," that is, his mansion at the foot of the hill, where he could get his provisions easily, and see the world as it flowed along the road. In an old German village there is accordingly to be found generally a somewhat stately mansion below as well as the castle above, with the same coat-of-arms carved over their doors, inhabited by the same family in past times, oscillating as circumstances required between the house and the castle.

When roads were maintained and the post-horses found by the knights and barons, they could charge for their toll enough to cover the expense of entertainment; but it is not improbable that the servant, the butler, received a present which he transmitted to his master, and which the traveller reckoned as a fair remuneration for the wine he had drunk and the meat and bread he had eaten.

The lords house could always be recognized by the shield with his arms hung up over his door, and to this day the signboard is in German "Schild." The sign was always armorial. In many a Tyrolean and in some old German inns may still be seen the coat-of-arms of the noble owner, now plain publican, carved in front of the inn, and the schild—the heraldic shield with lion, or eagle, or bear, or swan, or ape, or hare—hanging as well from a richly ornamented iron bar.

Nothing can be conceived more picturesque than the one long street of Sterzing on the Brenner Pass: the houses are old, gabled, and a considerable number of them have their stanchions of richly twisted ironwork painted and gilt, hanging out on each side over the narrow street, supporting large shields with armorial beasts. In the church may be seen the same shields on monuments, crowned with baronial coronets and knightly helmets, the tombstones of former owners and inhabitants of these houses, and also of former landlords.

As commerce increased, and the roads became better, it was impossible for the nobles to entertain freely. Moreover, the Thirty Years' War, again the Seven Years' War, and finally the Napoleonic wars, had so impoverished them that they were forced to charge for entertainment, and to derive a revenue from it.

From one cause or another they lost their land, and then sank to be mere innkeepers. This was rarely the case in Germany, but it was not uncommon in Tyrol, where to this day the hotel and tavern keepers represent the best blood in the land. They have well-attested pedigrees, of which they are proud; and they dispense hospitality, not now gratuitously, but with courtesy and kindliness, in the very houses in which their ancestors have lived for three or four hundred years, and under the sign which adorned the helmets and shields of their forefathers when they rode in tournament or battle.

At the Krone, the principal inn at Brunecken, in the Puster Thal, the staircase is adorned with the portraits of the family, containing among them prelates, and warriors, and stately ladies; and the homely Tyrolese girl in costume who attends you at table, and the quiet, simple old host and hostess are the lineal descendants of these grandees.

The writer spent a night at the homeliest of taverns at Eben, between the Aachen See and Jenbach. The little parlour was perfectly plain, panelled with brown pine, with a bench round it; in one corner a rude crucifix, in another the pottery-stove. The host wore a brown jacket and knee-breeches, and a coarse knitted cap on his head—quite a peasant, to all appearance, yet he could show his pedigree in an emblazoned tree, and right to bear arms as an adeliger. So, also, at the Croce at Cortina d' Ampezzo. The family tree adorns the passage of the humble inn, and a few years ago, before the run of tourists to the Dolomites, the pretty newly married hostess wore the local costume. On the post road between Nauders and Meran, the last station where the diligence stops before reaching Meran is at an inn, the sign of which is the "Brown Bear." The arms of the family are carved on the front of the house, and the sign hangs over the door. The landlord represents the family which bore these arms in mediæval times, and he is, I believe, of baronial rank.

Mals, in the same valley, stands at the junction of the road from Italy over the Stelvio, and that to Nauders, and that to Meran, as also the road up the Münster Thal, which likewise leads to Italy. Down to last century it was, no doubt, an important place. Trade flowed through it. There are remains of castles and towers about it, and in the Middle Ages several noble families held these castles, the keys to Germany from Italy, under the Emperor. The place lies somewhat high, the land is not very productive, and they were not able to become rich on the yield of the soil. They lived on the tolls they took of travellers, and when the postal system was established and passed into the hands of Government, they lost a source of revenue, and went down in the world. At Mals are two or three inns, and two or three general stores. At the latter can be bought anything, from ready-made clothes to sheets of notepaper and sealing-wax. The principal of these stores is held by a family named Flora. It is worth the while of the traveller to turn into the cemetery of the parish church, and he will find ranges of white marble tombs of the family of his host at the inn, and of the Floras, where he has bought some notepaper and a reel of cotton. These tombs are sculptured with baronial helmets, and proud marshalling of heraldic serpents and bears, with impalements and quarterings and achievements—I will not be certain, but I think they have supporters also.

I remember that in Messrs. Churchill and Babington's charming book on the Dolomites they speak with astonishment at finding themselves in an inn which was once a noble family's residence, and then discovering that they were the guests of this noble family; but such a state of things is by no means uncommon in Tyrol. There are hundreds of innkeepers who are of noble rank, with a right to wear coronets, and who do assume them—on their tombstones.

Now, this state of things in Tyrol is peculiarly interesting, because it shows us a social condition which has passed into oblivion everywhere else, and of which, among ourselves, the only reminiscenses are to be found in the heraldic signs of inns, and in the host being termed landlord. The lord of the manor ceased to be landlord of inn with us a long time ago, and probably very early put in a substitute to act as host, and kept himself aloof from his guests. He lived in his manor-house, and entertained at a guest-house, a hostelry. In a good many instances in England, where there is a great house, the servants of guests are accommodated at the manorial inn, by the park gates. It was not so in Tyrol, and to this day the evidence of this old custom remains. As already said, in Tyrol one may be entertained by the curé. This is only where there is no inn. Where the lord did not have a mansion and receive, there the pastor received in his parsonage. Now, in England there is scarcely a parish without its church inn—an inn generally situated on the glebe, of which the parsonis the owner; and very often this church inn is a great cause of vexation to him. It stands close to the church—sometimes conspicuously taken out of the churchyard—and the proximity is not often satisfactory. The church inn has for its sign, may be, the "Ring of Bells," or simply the "Bell," or the "Lamb and Flag"—anyhow, some sign that points to its connection with the church. These inns were originally the places of entertainment where the parson supplied the wants of the parishioners who came from a distance, and brought their food with them, but not their drink. These people attended morning service, then sat in the church house, or church inn, and ate their meal, and were supplied with ale by the parson or his substitute.

At Abbotskerswell, South Devon, is a perfect old church inn, that has remained untouched from, probably, the reign of Richard II. It consists of two rooms—one above stairs, and one below. The men sat in the lower, the women in the upper room. Each was furnished with an enormous fire in winter, and here the congregation took their dinner before attending vespers.

In France the same thing took place in the church porches, and that was one reason why the porches were made so large. Great abuses were consequent, and several of the French bishops charged against, and the Councils condemned, the eating and drinking in the porches.

If the people from a distance were to remain for the afternoon service, they must go somewhere. The writer has seen the porches of German and French cathedrals full of women eating their dinner, after having heard the morning mass, and who were waiting for the service in the afternoon; but they are no longer served there with ale and wine by the clergy. Flodoard, in his account of S. Remigius, says that that saint could only stop the inveterate custom at Rheims by a miracle: he made all the taps of those who supplied the wine to stop running. But to return once more to the ordinary tavern. The French auberge, the Italian albergo, derive from the old Teutonic here-berga, which has for signification "the lord's shelter"—that is, the house of shelter provided by the lord of the manor.

A cartulary of 1243, published in the Gallia Christiana, shows us a certain knight Raimond, who, on his birthday, assigns an annual charge on his estate of three hundred sous for the support of the village hostelry, which shows us that in France the nobles very early gave up themselves entertaining, but considered themselves in some way bound to keep up the inn.

In 1380, at Liège, the clergy stirred up the people against the nobles to obtain their expulsion. But a difficulty arose, as it was found that the nobles were the innkeepers of the city, and to expel them was to close the public-houses, and for that the Liègeois were not prepared. So the riot came to an abrupt conclusion.

In Farquhar's Beaux' Stratagem, 1707, the squire is represented as habitually frequenting his village inn, and as habitually becoming drunk there. Smollett tells us that Squire Pickle, when he retired into the country, met with abundance of people who, in consideration of his fortune, courted his acquaintance, and breathed nothing but friendship and hospitality; yet even the trouble of receiving and returning these civilities was an intolerable fatigue to a man of his habits and disposition. He therefore left the care of the ceremonial to his sister, who indulged herself in all the pride of formality, while he himself, having made a discovery of a public-house in the neighbourhood, went thither every evening, and enjoyed his pipe and can, being well satisfied with the behaviour of the landlord, whose communicative temper was a great comfort to his own taciturnity. At the village tavern squire and attorney and doctor were wont to meet, and not infrequently the parson appeared there as well. That condition of affairs is past. It is not so in Germany—where, in small villages, gentlefolks and tradesmen, the Catholic priest and the evangelical pastor, the baron and the notary, the grocer and the surgeon, meet of an evening, knock glasses, rub ideas, and in a cloud of tobacco smoke lose bigotry in religion and class prejudice. Would not the same have been the case had our squires and parsons continued to frequent the village inn? Would not their presence have acted as a check on over much drinking?

It is now too late to revert to old habits, but I have a hankering notion that it would have been, perhaps, on the whole, better if the gentle classes had not "cut" the tavern, and instead have taken their ease there, in sobriety and kindly intercourse, yeoman, squire, and farm labourer, on the one level of the tavern floor, round the blaze of the one hearth warming all, drinking the same generous liquor, and in the one mellowing atmosphere of tobacco smoke.

CHAPTER VIII

Every manor had its mill, and consequently there is hardly a village without one. The lord of the manor had certain rights over the mill and over his tenants, who were required to go to his mill and to no other.

The mill is usually a very picturesque adjunct to the scenery. It is frequently an old building; it has ancient trees standing round it; there is the mill-pool, the sluice, the wheel, and the foaming waters discharged over it.

The miller himself is a genial figure, dusted with flour, his face lighted up with the consciousness that though all the rest of the parish may starve, that will not he.

And the miller's cottage is almost always scrupulously clean and well-kept. I have known many mills, but I never knew a slattern among miller's wives, never saw a hug-a-mug condition of affairs in the miller's home.

The miller anciently did not stand over-well with the rest of the villagers. He ground the corn of the farmer and the gleanings of the poor, and took his toll from each sack, his fist full and more than his due, so it was said. The millers thumb was a big thumb, and his fist had a large grip.

But it was not only that the miller was supposed to take more than his due of grain, he was suspected of taking what was not his from the lips of the girls and wives who came with their sacks of corn to the mill to have it ground. The element of jealousy of the miller breaks out in a great many country songs. The good nature, the joviality, the cleanness of the miller, no doubt made him a persona grata to the fair sex in a village, and those who could not rival him revenged themselves in lame poems and halting song.

But for all that he was regarded with suspicion, there was a sense of something picturesque, romantic about the miller. He was a type of the genial, self-reliant Englishman; and the writer of the well-known song of the Miller of Dee hit him off to a nicety:—

"There was a jolly miller once lived by the River Dee;
He worked and sang from morn till night; no lark more
blithe than he;
And this the burden of his song for ever used to be,
I care for nobody, no, not I, if nobody cares for me."

That the miller is esteemed to be a shrewd man appears from such songs and plays as the "Miller of Mansfield."

So also the miller's daughter forms a topic for many a story, play and song, never with a sneer, always spoken of with admiration, not only because she is goodly, but a type of neatness, and "cleanliness comes next to goodliness." The new machinery and steam are fast displacing the old mills that were turned by water, and the old dusty miller is giving place to the trim gentleman who does most of the work in the office, without whitening his coat.

I know an aged miller and his wife who had been for years occupying a quaint old-fashioned mill of the simplest construction, and which answered all purposes required in the village. But a few years ago a new venture was started—a great mill worked by steam, and with electric lighting through it, and now no corn is sent to the ancient mill that is crumbling and rotting away, and the old people are decaying within it.

"Thomas," said I one evening over the fire to this miller, "how long have you been married?"

"Fifty years next Michaelmas."

"And when did you court your wife? When did you find the right one?"

"Lor bless y', sir, I can't mind the time when we weren't courting each other. I b'lieve us began as babbies. Us knowed each other as long as us knowed anything at all. Us went to school together—us larned our letters together, us was vaccinated together, her was took from my arm; and us growed up together."

"And when did you first think of making her yours?"

"Bless y', sir, I never first thought on it at all; I never thought other from the time I began to think but that it must be—it wor ordained so."

"Have you children?"

69

"Yes; they be all out in the world and doing well. We haven't to blush for any of them—men and maids all alike—respectable."

"Then you ought to be very happy."

"I reckon us ought, and us should be but for that new mill."

"It is spoiling your custom?"

"It is killin' of us old folks out. It isn't so much that us gets no grinding I mind, but it leaves me and my Anne with no means in our old age, and us don't like to go on to the childer, and us don't like to go into the work'us. There it is. Us did reckon on being able honestly to get our bread for ourselves and ax nobody for nothing. But now this ere new mill wi' the steam ingens and the electric light—someone must pay for all that, and who is that but the customers? I've no electric light here, water costs nothing. Coals costs twenty-one shillings a ton, and ittakes a deal o' coals to make the ingen march. Who pays for the coals? Who pays for the electric light? The customers get the flour at the same price as I send it out with none of them jangangles. How do they manage it? I reckon the corn is tampered with—there's white china-clay or something put wi' the flour. It can't be done otherwise. But I reckon folk like to say, 'Our flour comed from that there mill worked wi' steam and lighted by electric light,' and if they have those things, then, I say they can't have pure flour. So it must be, I think, but folk say that I am an old stoopid and don't understand nothing. All I can say is I can turn out wholesome flour, and niver put nothing in but corn grains, and niver turned out nothing but corn flour, wheat and oat and barley."

On the day of the golden wedding of the old couple I visited them. I made a point of this, and brought them some little comfort.

I found them very happy. A son and a daughter had taken a holiday to see their parents and congratulate them. The parson's wife had sent in a plum pudding, the squire a bottle of old port. Several friends had remembered them—even the miller in the new style, who had electric light and steam power, had contributed a cake. There were nuts and oranges—but perhaps the present which gave most gratification was a doll, a miller with a floured face, sent by a grandchild with a rough scrawl. I supply the stops to make it intelligible.

"Dear Grandada and Granny,—At skool, teacher said old

pipple go into a sekond childood. So has you be so tremenjous old you must be orful babies. I think you will want a doll, so i sends you wun, with mutch love, and i drest the doll myself as a miller. Hever yors, dear grandada and granny.—Rosie."

Though the village mill usually—almost always—presents a pleasant picture in one's memory, a picture of cheerfulness and content, of good nature and neatness, it is not always so. I remember one mill which carries with it a sadness whenever I recall it. Not that the mill was gloomy in itself, but that the story connected with it was such as to make one sad.

The miller, whom we will call Pike, was unhappily somewhat inclined to drink. He was not an intemperate man at home, far from it; and in his mill, at his work, he was always sober. But when he went to market, when he got among boon companions, he was unable to resist the temptation of taking more than was good for his head. He did a very respectable business, and turned over a good deal of money, and was altogether a "warm" man. One day he went to market and gathered in there several debts that were owing him, and put all his money, amounting to twenty-five pounds seventeen and sixpence, in a pouch of leather, tied a bit of string round the neck, put it in his pocket—that of his overcoat as it happened, and not in his trousers or his breast pocket—and, mounting his tax cart, drove home.

The evening had closed in, and part of his way was through a wood, where the shadows lay thick and inky. Whether it were that he had drunk too much or that the road was too dark to see his way well, I cannot say, but it is certain that the miller was upset and flung into the hedge.

Just then up came a workman, a man named Richard Crooke, who caught the horse, righted the cart, and helped Pike, the miller, into his seat again. Pike was shaken but not hurt. He was confused in his mind, not, however, so much so as to fail to know who had assisted him, and to thank him for it.

On reaching home he at once put up his horse, and entering his house, and going upstairs, took off his overcoat, found it was torn and in a shocking condition of dirt, wherefore he threw it aside and went to bed.

He slept till late next morning, and when he woke he remembered

71

but uncertainly the events of the previous evening. However, after he had had a cup of strong tea made for him by his mother—he was a widower without children, and his mother kept house for him—he began to recall events more distinctly, and then, with a start, he remembered his money bag. He hastily ran upstairs to the torn and soiled overcoat and felt in all the pockets. The bag of gold and silver was gone.

In a panic Pike rushed out of the house and ran to the scene of his accident. He searched there wherever there were tokens of the upset, and they were plain in the mud and the bruised twigs of the bushes. Not a trace of the bag that contained so much money could he find, not one ha'penny out of the twenty-five pounds seventeen shillings and sixpence did he recover.

He went to Crooke's cottage to question him. The man was out. He was horseman to one of the farmers, so Pike pursued him to the farm and found him ploughing. He asked him if he had seen— picked up anything. No—Crooke had not observed anything. Indeed, as he remarked, the night was too dark, and the blackness under the trees was too complete for him to have seen anything that had been dropped. Crooke seemed somewhat nettled at being questioned. Of course, had he noticed anything belonging to the miller fallen out of his trap, or out of his pockets, he would have handed it to the owner.

Pike was not satisfied. He was convinced that no one had been over the by-road that morning before he examined it, as it led only to the mill and to the farm where Crooke worked.

What had become of the money? Had anyone retained it?

Not long afterwards, to the astonishment of the miller and some of the farmers, Crooke bought a little property, a cottage and a couple of fields. There was no doubt that he had borrowed some of the money requisite; he said he had saved the rest. Was that possible? From that moment a strong and ineradicable conviction formed in Pike's mind that he had been robbed by Richard Crooke.

With envy and rage he watched the husbandman move into his little tenement, and begin to till his field. Pike considered that this tenement was his own by rights. Crooke had bought it with the miller's money taken from him on the night when he was upset. Crooke had taken advantage of his being a little fresh, and a little

72

confused by the fall, to purloin the bag containing twenty-five pounds seventeen shillings and sixpence.

From this time all joy, all cheeriness was gone from the life of the miller; his heart turned bitter as gall, and all his bitterness was directed against Richard Crooke. He brooded over his wrong. He did not venture openly to accuse the man he suspected, but he dropped hints which prejudiced opinion against Crooke. But everyone knew that this Richard had been a careful man, saving his money.

Pike watched the corn grow on Crooke's field; he wished a blight might fall upon it. But it throve, the ears were heavy, it was harvested in splendid condition, and stacked in the corner of the field.

Then, one night the corn rick was on fire. This was the work of an incendiary. It must have been done wilfully, and by someone who bore Crooke a grudge. Richard had not insured, and the loss to him was a very serious matter. It might have been ruin had not a "brief" been got up and some pounds subscribed to relieve him.

No one could say who had done the deed. Yet nobody doubted who the incendiary had been. Nothing could be proved against anyone.

A twelvemonth passed. A malevolent pleasure had filled the heart of the miller when he had heard that Crooke's stack was consumed, and he somewhat ostentatiously gave half a sovereign to the brief. He was angry and offended when the half-sovereign was returned him. Richard Crooke declined to receive his contribution.

During the year Pike's character deteriorated; he went more frequently to the public-house, he neglected his work, and what he did was done badly.

Then one morning—on opening his eyes in bed, they fell on a little recess in the wall, high up beyond most people's reach, a place where he had been wont to put away things he valued and did not desire should be meddled with. A sudden thought, a suspicion, flashed across his mind. He started from bed, put his hand into the recess, and drew forth his money bag, opened it and counted out twenty-five pounds seventeen shillings and sixpence.

On returning home, the night of his accident, he had taken the bag out of his torn and sullied overcoat pocket, had put it in this hiding-place, and forgotten all about it. He hastily dressed himself—he would eat no breakfast, but drank brandy, several glasses full—went out, and when next seen was a corpse, dragged out of his mill-pond, hugging his money bag.

Not till then were mouths unlocked, and men said that Pike, angered at his loss, believing that Crooke had robbed him, had fired the stack; and that when he found out his mistake, in shame and remorse, and uncertain how he could remedy the wrong done—he had destroyed himself.

CHAPTER IX

As the sun to the planets so stands the manor-house to the farms on the manor; that is to say, so far as the relations of dignity and dependence go. But the sun gives to its satellites and receives nothing, whereas from the lord of the manor come the loan of land, of house, and of farm-buildings, for which loan the tenant pays a rent, that is to say, so much interest on so much capital placed at his disposal. An old English farmhouse that has not been meddled with is a very interesting study. It represents to us the type of our manor-houses before the reign of the Tudors. Owing to the prosperity which England enjoyed at the cessation of the Wars of the Roses our gentry rebuilt their houses, and rebuilt yet again, as fashions changed, so that we have very few of the manor-houses left that were erected before Tudor times.

The old farmhouse in England is in plan very much what the old manoir was in France. I will take a plan and give a drawing of that of Anseremme on the Meuse near Dinant. This has the parish church attached to it, as it not infrequently was to the manor-house in England.

The dwelling-house forms one side of the courtyard. The other sides are occupied by farm-buildings, stables, cart-sheds, granaries, etc.

To reach the front door of the house one must wade through straw trampled by cattle and oozing with manure. Our forefathers did not mind that. Our farmers of the right sort love it. A farmer whose heart does not glow at stable and cowstall manure has missed his vocation. But everything in its place, and the unfortunate feature of this paving of manure was that it adhered to boots and entered the house. This mattered little when halls were strewn with rushes. But when polished oak boards and next carpets came in, the entrance to the house had to be altered, so that at least the women-kind need not tread over ankles in manure before entering the house.

Where there is a farmhouse there must be a court in which the cattle can run, and where better than under the eye of the master and mistress.

But there was, and is, another, and more serious, drawback. Wells have been sunk close to the houses, and very generally in intimate relation to the courtyard. The result is that in a great many cases the water in the wells becomes contaminated. It is really amazing how many centuries have rolled by without people discovering the fact that such proximity produces contamination, and such contamination leads to diphtheria, or typhoid fever. But stupidity is ever with us, so I do not wonder. Here is a fact. In a certain village of over a thousand inhabitants, that I knew, there is a National School, which having an endowment commands the services of a first-class schoolmaster.

Now it fell out that water from a beautiful spring among the hills was brought into this village, and a tap placed outside the schoolmasters residence.

Said the village schoolmaster to himself, "If I use this water I shall have to pay the rate. If I don't I cannot be called upon for it. I will get all my water from the well in the adjoining farmyard." He did so, and his young wife and child died of diphtheria.

Now, if a man like a cultured schoolmaster at the close of the nineteenth century will act like this, is it a marvel that our forefathers, who were without the means of knowing better, should have made such mistakes?

A merciful Providence must have brooded over our ancestors and protected them; how else is it possible that they were not all swept away, and none left to be the progenitors of our own enlightened selves?

I suppose that systems adapted themselves to their surroundings and to what they assimilated, and our forbears got into the way of fattening and thriving on bacilli, germs, and all like horrors.

But to return to the farmhouse.

In one that is well-conducted, the court in which pigs wallow, bullocks poach the litter, ducks waddle, and find nutriment in what would be death to all other creatures, is the nucleus and treasury, the cream of the whole farm. Having considered the plan of the Walloon Manoir, look at a plan of an old English farm congeries of buildings. Is it not clear that—omitting the church—the type is the same?

The old-fashioned farmer, like the old-fashioned squire, did not ask to have a view of distant horizons from his windows, but sought to look upon his stock and see that it throve.

It was, may be, more riskful to leave cattle about in the fields in former days, though I am not very sure of that. England was always a quiet, law-abiding, well-conducted country. And perhaps the cattle at one time may have been driven into the pen for the night, about the masters house. His court was his kraal. But that was long, long ago, when there were wolves and cattle-lifters in the land. In ordered times only ewes at lambing time, and cows about to calve, and young bullocks were kept in the courtyard; and the calves that the dairymaid had to feed, by dipping her hand in milk and then giving it to the long-legged, silly creatures to suck.

The cows were milked in the fields, and milked by the dairymaids. Then that fashion was abandoned, and cows were driven to the stables to be there milked, and these cowhouses were so deep in manure as to dirty the skirts and white stockings of the maids, so they withdrew from the task, and now only men milk the cows.

Alas for the dairymaid! That charming, merry, innocent ideal of a country girl. Indeed to be a milkmaid and to be merry were almost synonymous in the olden time. Sir Thomas Overbury, in his "Character of a Milkmaid," says: "She dares go alone, and unfold her sheep in the night, and fears no manner of ill, because she means none; yet, to say truth, she is never alone: she is still accompanied with old songs, honest thoughts, and prayers, but short ones."

In the "Character of a Ballad-monger," in Whimzies, 1631, we find: "Stale ballad news, cashiered the city, must now ride fast for the country, where it is no less admired than a giant in a pageant: till at last it grows so common there, too, as every poor milkmaid can chant and chirp it under her cow, which she useth as a harmless charm to make her let down her milk."

In Beaumont and Fletcher's play, The Coxcomb, Nan, the Milkmaid, says:

> "Come, you shall e'en home with me, and be our fellow;
> Our home is so honest!
> And we serve a very good woman, and a gentlewoman;
> And we live as merrily, and dance o' good days
> After evensong. Our wake shall be on Sunday:

77

Do you know what a wake is?—we have mighty cheer then."

Who does not remember old Isaac Walton and his merry ballad-singing dairymaid?

Pepys, in his Diary, 13th October, 1662, writes: "With my father took a melancholy walk to Portholme, seeing the country-maids milking their cows there, they being there now at grass; and to see with what mirth they come all home together in pomp with their milk, and sometimes they have music go before them."

> "When cold bleak winds do roar,
> And flowers can spring no more,
> The fields that were seen
> So pleasant and green
> By winter all candied o'er:
> Oh! how the town lass
> Looks, with her white face
> And lips so deadly pale.
> But it is not so
> With those that go
> Through frost and snow,
> With cheeks that glow,
> To carry the milking pail."

On May-day was the festival of the milkmaids. I can remember, in 1845, seeing Jack in the Green and Maid Marian parading in the Strand.

Pepys, in his Diary, on the 1st May, 1667, enters—"To Westminster; on the way meeting many milkmaids with their garlands upon their pails, dancing with a fiddler before them."

In a set of prints called "Tempest's Cryes of Lon'on," one is called "The Merry Milkmaid," whose proper name was Kate Smith. She is dancing with her milk-pail on her head, decorated with silver cups, tankards, and salvers, borrowed for the purpose, and tied together with ribbands, and ornamented with flowers. "Of later years, the plate, with other decorations, were placed in a pyramidical form, and carried by two chairmen upon a wooden horse. The milkmaids walked before it, and performed the dance without any encumbrance."

In a curious German account of London and London life, written by

78

Otto Von Rosenberg, and published at Leipzig in 1834, is a picture of a milkmaids' May dance; but in London it had become a chimney-sweeps' performance in place of one of milkmaids. In the country it maintained its character as a festival of dairymaids. Rosenberg thus describes it:

"A hobbledehoy youth leads the procession with a three-cornered cocked hat on his head, pasted over with gilt paper. Eyebrows and cheeks are strongly marked with paint. A coat of gay colour flaps about his body, and this coat is imitated from the uniform of a French field-marshal, and is sown over with flowers and ornaments of gilt paper. Over his right shoulder hangs a red silk band, to which a wooden sword is attached. His knee-breeches and stockings are white. He is followed by a figure from head to toe buried under a conical structure, which is woven round with fresh may, and at the summit has a crown. This object has no other purport than to hobble after the rest.

"To complete the trefoil is a girl who stands in no way behind Netherland damsels in beauty and lively movements. Her hair, which in the morning had been carefully done up in braids, becomes disengaged by the action and heat, and her incessant leaps and twirls, and finally falls about her shoulders like that of a fury. She wears a low dress and short sleeves of white very transparent texture reaching to her calves, and exposing below rather massive feet, which are wound about with green. In her hand she waves a great wooden spoon, and this she extends to the windows for gratuities. But as she dances through the streets she brandishes this great spoon above her head, like a witch who is invoking a spirit."[6]

Alack-a-day! The milkmaid is a creature of the past. Now in farmhouses there is great difficulty in getting any girl to work. They want to go to the towns, or consider themselves too highly educated to do menial work.

And the sower, the mower, the reaper and thrasher are also extinct.

I remember as a boy repeatedly watching a sower pacing up and down a field strewing the corn to right and left from the wooden seed-lap carried in front, and thinking what a picture it made. Now corn is sown with a drill.

In the very early morning, as the sun rose and the dew was on the

---

[6] Bilder aus London, Leipzig, 1834.

grass, it was pleasant of old to hear the musical whetting of the scythe, and then the hiss as the blade swept through the herb and shore it down. That is no more. The grass is mown in the meadows by the mechanical mower, and on the lawn by a contrivance whose movements are anything but musical. In former days also the harvesting was a real delight. The reapers, with their hooks, worked their way along in rows. It cannot be better described than in the Harvest Song, well known in the south-west of England:

"The corn is all ripe, and the reapings begin,
The fruits of the earth, O we gather them in;
At morning so early the reap-hooks we grind,
And away to the fields for to reap and to bind;
The foreman goes first in the hot summer glow,
And he sings with a laugh, my lads, all of a row.
Then, all of a row! then all of a row!
And to-night we will sing boys All of a row!

"We're in, says the catchpole, behind and before,
We'll have a fresh edge and a sheaf or two more.
The master stands back for to see us behind;
Well done, honest fellow's, bring the sheaves to the bind.
Well done, honest fellows, pare up your first brink,
You shall have a fresh edge, and a half pint to drink.
Then, all of a row! etc.

"And so we go through the heat of the day,
Some reaping, some binding, all merry and gay.
We'll reap and we'll bind, we will whistle and sing,
Unflagging until the last sheaf we bring in.
It's all our enjoyment wherever we go,
To work and to sing, Brothers, all of a row.
Then, all of a row! etc.

"Our day's work is done, to the farmhouse we steer,
To eat a good supper and drink humming beer;
We wish the good farmer all blessings in life,
And drink to his health, and as well to his wife.
God prosper the grain for next harvest we sow,
When again in the arrish we'll sing, Boys, hallo!
Then, all in a row! etc."

When the reapers had cut nearly the whole field they reached a portion that had been purposely left, and this, instead of attacking in row, they surrounded, shouting "A neck! a neck!" and of this the last sheaf was fashioned, and on top of it was a little figure formed of plaited corn, and this was conveyed in triumph to the garner.

My old coachman, who had served three generations of my family and had seen four, was the last man who made these corn-men in our neighbourhood, and long after the custom had been abandoned, he was wont on every harvest thanksgiving to produce one of these comical figures for suspension in the church. The head was made of a tuft of barley, and flowers were interwoven with the rest.

All this is of the past, and so also is the throb of the flail. There are not many labourers now who understand how to wield the flail. The steam thrasher travels from farm to farm and thrashes and winnows, relieving man of the labour. The flail is only employed for the making of "reed," i.e., straw for thatching the rick.

What a robust, rubicund, hearty fellow is our old English farmer. The breed is not extinct, thank God! At one time, when it was the fashion to run two and three farms into one, and let this conglomerate to a man reputed warm and knowing, then it did seem as if the "leather pocketed" farmer was doomed to extinction. But it is the gentleman farmer who has gone to pieces, and the simple old type has stood the brunt of the storm, and has weathered the bad times.

What a different man altogether he is from the French paysan and the German bauer! The latter, among the mountains, is a fine specimen, his wealth is in oxen and cows. But the bauer, on arable land in the plains, is an anxious, worn man, who falls into the hands of the Jews, almost inevitably. Ourfarmers, well fed, open-hearted, hospitable, yet close-fisted over money, would do well to learn a little thrift from the continental peasant. On market days, if they sell and buy, they also spend a good deal at the ordinary and in liquor.

At a tythe dinner I gave, in another part of England from that I now occupy, the one topic of conversation and debate was whether it were expedient on returning from market to tumble into the ditch or into the hedge, and if it should happen that the accident happened in the road, at what portion of the highway it was "plummest" to fall.

On market days is the meeting of the Board of Guardians, and on that Board the farmer exercises authority and rules.

81

An old widow in receipt of parish relief once remarked: "Our pass'n hev been preachin' this Michaelmas a deal about the angels bein' our guardgins. Lork a biddy! I've been in two counties, in Darset and Zummerset, as well as here. Guardgins be guardgins whereiver they be. And I knows very well, if them angels is to be our guardgins in kingdom come—it'll be a loaf and 'arf a crown and no more for such as we."

In North Devon there was a farmer, whom we will call Tickle, who was on a certain Board of Guardians, of which Lord P. was chairman. Now Mrs. Tickle died, and so for a week or two the farmer did not take his usual seat. The chairman got a resolution passed condoling with Mr. Tickle on his loss.

Next Board day, the farmer appeared, whereupon Lord P. addressed him: "It is my privilege, duty, and pleasure, Mr. Tickle, to convey to you, on behalf of your brother guardians, an expression of our sincere and heartfelt and profound regret for the sad loss you have been called on to endure. Mr. Tickle, the condolence that we offer you is most genuine, sir. We feel, all of us, that the severance which you have had to undergo is the most painful and supreme that falls to man's lot in this vale of tears. Mr. Tickle, it is at once a rupture of customs that have become habitual, a privation of an association the sweetest, holiest, and dearest that can be cemented on earth, and it is—it is—in short—it is—Mr. Tickle, we condole with you most cordially."

The farmer addressed looked about with a puzzled and vacant expression, then rubbed his chin, then his florid cheeks, and seemed thoroughly nonplussed. Presently a brother farmer whispered in his ear, "Tes all about the ou'd missus you've lost."

"Oh!" and the light of intelligence illumined his face, "that's it, es it. Well, my lord and genl'men, I thank y' kindly all the same, but my ou'd woman—her wor a terr'ble teasy ou'd toad. It hev plased the Lord to take 'er, and plase the Lord he'll keep 'er."

The ordinary farmer is not a reader—how can he be, when he is out of doors all day, and up in the morning before daybreak? We complain that he does not advance with the times; but he is a cautious man, who makes quite sure of his ground before he steps.

The County Council, at the expense of the ratepayers, send about lecturers, who are well paid, to hold forth in village schoolrooms on scientific agriculture, the chemistry of the soil, and scientific dairying.

No one usually attends these lectures except a few ladies, but on one occasion a farmer was induced by the rector or the squire, as a personal favour, to listen to one on the chemistry of common life.

He listened with attention when the lecturer described the constituents of the atmosphere, oxygen, hydrogen, nitrogen. At the close he stood up, stretched himself, and said: "Muster lecturer! You've told us a terr'ble lot about various soorts o' gins, oxegen and so on, I can't mind 'em all, but you ha'nt mentioned the very best o' all in my 'umble experience, and that's Plymouth gin. A drop o' that with suggar and water—hot—the last thing afore you go to bed, not too strong nor too weak neither, is the very first-ratedst of all. I've tried it for forty years."

And then he went forth, shrugged his shoulders, and said, "That chap, he's traveller for some spirit merchants, as have some new-fangled gins—but I'll stick to Plymouth gin, I will."

A friend of mine was Mayor for a year in a town, the name of which is unimportant. Being of a hospitable and kindly turn, he sent invitations to all the farmers in the neighbourhood who were within the purlieu of the borough to dine with him on a certain evening, and at the bottom of the invitation put the conventional R. S. V. P.

To his surprise he received no answers whatever. The invitation, however, was much discussed at the ordinary, and the mysterious letters at the close subjected to scrutiny and debate.

"Now what do you makes 'em out to mane?" asked one farmer.

"Well, I reckon," answered he who was addressed, "tes what we're to ate at his supper. Rump Steak and Veal Pie."

"Git out for a silly," retorted the first, "muster bain't sach a vule as to have two mates on table to once. Sure enough them letters stand for Rump Steak and Viggy (plum) Pudden'."

"Ah! Seth! you have it. That's the truth," came in assent from the whole table.

But what a fine man the old farmer is—the very type of John Bull. That he is being driven out of existence by foreign colonial competition I cannot believe. He is a slow man to accommodate himself to changed circumstances, but he can turn himself about when he sees his way; and he has a shrewd head, and knows soil and climate.

In George Coleman's capital play, "The Heir at Law," Lady Daberly says to her son Dick, "A farmer!—and what's a farmer, my dear?"

To which Dick replies, "Why, an English farmer, mother, is one who supports his family, and serves his country by his industry. In this land of commerce, mother, such a character is always respectable."

CHAPTER X

The type of the old English cottage was—one room below for kitchen and every other purpose by day, and one room upstairs for repose at night for the entire family, and this reached by a stair like a ladder. Very poor quarters as we now consider, but relatively not poor when compared with the farms and manor-houses at the time when they were built.

And a vast number of our labourers' cottages date from two, three, and four hundred years ago; especially where built of stone or "cob." The latter is kneaded clay with straw in it. This makes a warm and excellent wall, and one that will endure for ever if only the top be kept dry. Brick cottages are later. Timber and plaster belong to the fifteenth and sixteenth centuries. The oak turns hard as iron and is perhaps more enduring than iron, for the latter is eaten through in time with rust.

That which is destroying the old cottage is not the tooth of time, but the insurance office, which imposes heavy rates on thatched buildings, and when the thatch goes and its place is taken by slate, the beauty of the cottage is gone. But generally, if a cottage that was thatched has to be slated, it is found that the timbers were not put up to bear the weight of slate, so have to be renewed, and then it is said by the agent, "Pull the whole thing down, it is not worth re-roofing. Build it afresh from the foundation." Then, in the place of a lovely old building with its windows under thatch, and the latter covering it soft and brown and warm as the skin of a mole, arises a piece of hideousness that is perhaps more commodious, but hardly so comfortable. I know that labourers who have been transferred from old "cob" cottages under thatch to new brick cottages under slate, complain bitterly that they are losers in coziness by the exchange, and that they suffer from cold in these trim and gaunt erections.

No cottages are more lovely than those that are tiled, when the tiles are old; and the Eastern Counties, if they lack the beauty of landscape of the West, and of the Welsh hills, and the Lake district, infinitely surpass them in the picturesqueness of their groups of cottages. Slate, it must be admitted, is only beautiful when mellowed by the growth over it of lichen; and some slate not even time can make other than ugly.

I have been reading Professor Fawcett's Economic Position of the British Labourer, and I note the following passage relative to our agricultural workmen: "Theirs is a life of incessant toil for wages too scanty to give them a sufficient supply even of the first necessaries of life. No hope cheers their monotonous career; a life of constant labour brings them no other prospect than that when their strength is exhausted they must crave as suppliant mendicants a pittance from parish relief. Many classes of labourers have still to work as long, and for as little remuneration as they received in past times; and one out of every twenty inhabitants of England is sunk so deep in pauperism that he has to be supported by parochial relief."

This is very interesting. Mr. Fawcett was, I believe, blind and resided in a town. No doubt he evolved this sad picture out of his interior consciousness. Beside it let me put some notes from my diary.

1896.	Dec.	25,	Christmas Day. Universal holiday.
	"	26,	Day after Christmas. No work done.
"	27,		Sunday.
"	28,		Monday, Bank Holiday; no work.
1897.	Jan.	1,	New Year's Day, General Holiday; no work.
	"	2,	Saturday; not full work.
"	3,		Sunday.
"	6,		Old Christmas Day. No work done.
"	9,		Saturday; not full work.
"	10,		Sunday.
"	11,		Excursion to Plymouth and pantomime. Half the workmen gone to the pantomime.
"	13,		Hounds met. All the men off running after them. Wages as usual.

Ten work-days out of twenty. I don't grudge it them. I rejoice over it with all my heart, but I cannot see that this quite jumps with Professor Fawcett's description. Of course it is not Christmas time all the year, but at other times are other festivals, flower shows, reviews, harvest festivals, club feasts, Bank Holidays, regattas, etc., etc., and my experience is that when there is anything to be seen the workmen go to see it and take their wives with them.

A few years ago there was a large bazaar given in my neighbourhood. I asked afterwards of the secretary and treasurer from whom most money was taken. The answer was, "From the young agricultural workmen. Squires didn't come, farmers didn't come—all too poor; but the young farm lads and lasses seemed to have gold in their purses and not to mind spending it."

Very glad to hear it I was, only I regretted that it was one class only that was well off and not the other two.

Now let us see whether my experience of the wages and housing of the labourers agrees with Professor Fawcett's picture. Here, where I live—and it was the same when I was in other parts of England (before the depression there)—the wages of the labourer was fourteen to fifteen shillings a week. For a comfortable cottage with over half an acre of garden he pays from £4 to £6 per annum, hardly sufficient to pay for keeping the cottage in repair, consequently it may be said that he has garden and half the house rent given to him. The garden is worth to him from £4 to £6 per annum. Consequently his receipts per annum may be reckoned at £42 or £48. He has to pay out of this into his club. He has nothing to pay in rates or taxes, or for his children's education; and if he has children, every son, on leaving school, till he marries brings in to him say 6s. to 12s. per week for his board, and his daughters go out into service and earn from £10 to £20 per annum as wages, and ought to remit some of this to their parents.

I am convinced that there is many a peasant proprietor abroad who would jump at the offer to be an English farm labourer.

I have spent ten years in collecting the folk songs of the West of England, and I have not come across one in which the agricultural labourer grumbles at his lot. On the contrary, their songs, the very outpouring of their hearts, are full of joy and happiness. Once, indeed, an old minstrel did say to me, "Did y' ever hear, sir, 'The Lament of the Poor Man?'"

I pricked up my ears. Now at last I was about to hear some socialistic sentiment, some cry of anguish of the oppressed peasant. "No," I answered, "never—sing it me."

And then I heard it. The lament of a man afflicted with a scolding wife. That alone made him poor, and that affliction is not confined to the dweller in the cottage.

87

Here and there we do come on miserable cottages—a disgrace to the land. But to whom do they belong? They have been erected on lives, or by squatters, and the landlords have no power over them. I know a certain village which is nearly all ruinous; but there all the ruinous cottages are held on lives. It is quite true that the landowner can force the holder of the tenure to put it in repair, but he is reluctant to put on the screw of the law, and he argues, "The houses were built to last three lives—no more. When they fall in to me, they will fall in altogether, and I will build decent, solid cottages in their place."

Over the squatter's cottage he has no control whatever.

Listen to the note of the agricultural, downtrodden labourer, his wail of anguish under the heel of the squire and farmer.

> "When the day's work is ended and over, he'll go
> To fair or to market to buy him a bow,
> And whistle as he walks, O! and shrilly too will sing,
> There's no life like the ploughboy's all in merry spring.
>
> "Good luck to the ploughboy, wherever he may be,
> A fair pretty maiden he'll take on his knee,
> He'll drink the nut-brown ale, and this song the lad will sing,
> O the ploughboy is happier than the noble or the king."

This is sung from one end of England to another, and always to the same very rude melody in a Gregorian tone, that shows it has expressed the sentiments of the ploughboy for at least two hundred years.

Listen again:

> "Prithee lend your jocund voices,
> For to listen we're agreed;
> Come sing of songs the choicest,
> Of the life the ploughboys lead
> There are none that live so merry
> As the ploughboy does in spring,
> When he hears the sweet birds whistle
> And the nightingales to sing.
>
> "In the heat of the daytime
> It's little we can do,

We will lie beside our oxen
For an hour, or for two.
On the banks of sweet violets
I'll take my noontide rest,
And it's I can kiss a pretty girl
As hearty as the best.

"O, the farmer must have seed, sirs,
Or I swear he cannot sow,
And the miller with his millwheel
Is an idle man also.
And the huntsman gives up hunting,
And the tradesman stands aside,
And the poor man bread is wanting,
So 'tis we for all provide."

That last verse is delicious. It lets us into the very innermost heart of the ploughman. He knows his own value—God bless him. And so do we.

There is one great advantage in our English system, that, not being bound to the soil, the poor workman can go wherever there is a demand for him. And this is one reason why we have so many examples of a young fellow who rises high up in the social scale, and from being a poor lad springs to be a rich man.

In another chapter I shall have something to say of the parish ne'er-do-weel. But if every parish has one of these latter, there is hardly one that cannot show his contrary. And now for a true story of one of these latter.

There is no country in the world, America possibly excepted, where greater facilities are afforded for a youth of energy and intelligence to make his way. But there is something more that gives a lad now a chance of rising, something far less generally diffused than intelligence and less conspicuous than energy, which is in immense demand, and at a premium—and that is honesty. In ancient Greece the churlish philosopher is said to have lit a lamp and gone about the streets by day looking for an honest man. It is, perhaps, the failing of advanced and widespread culture that it encourages mental at the expense of moral progress; nay, further, that with the development of mental advance there is moral retrogression. Every man is now in such a hurry to make himself comfortable that he loses all scruple as to the way in which he sets about it, and so misses the one way paramount over all others, that of common honesty.

This lack of integrity is the thing that all employers complain of. They can no longer repose trust in their workmen, in their clerks— all have to be watched. There is no question as to their abilities, only as to their honesty.

This leads me to tell the story—which is true—of a young man with whose career I am well acquainted, from childhood till he was prematurely cut off whilst in the ripeness of his powers, trusted, esteemed, and loved by all with whom he was brought in contact. He began life with little to favour him. His father was a quarryman who was killed by a fall of rock, and his mother died not long after, never having recovered from the shock of the loss of a dearly loved young husband. So the orphan boy was left to be brought up by his grandmother, a widow, who went out charing for her maintenance, and who received eighteen pence and a loaf per week from the parish, and who is alive to this day.

The lad grew up lanky, and looked insufficiently fed. The squire of the parish took him early into his service to clean boots and run errands at sixpence a day, and after a while, as the fellow proved trusty, advanced him to be a butler boy in the house, in livery, to clean knives and attend the door.

Trusty and good the lad remained in this condition also, but it was not congenial to him. One day the housemaid told the mistress, with a laugh, "Please, ma'am, what do you think? Every now and then I've found bits of wood laid one across another under Richard's bed. I couldn't make out what it meant, at last I've found out. He's made an arrangement with the gardener on certain mornings to be up very early before his regular work begins, that he may go round the greenhouses with himand help him there, and a bit in the gardens. Richard won't be a minute late for his work in the house, but he do so dearly love to be in the garden that he'll get up at four o'clock to go there, and as he's a heavy sleeper, he has the notion that if he makes a little cross under his bed by putting one stick across another, and says over it, 'I want to be waked at four o'clock,' then sure enough at that hour he will rise."

When his master and mistress knew the lad's taste, and heard from him how much happier he would be in the gardens than in the house, they put him with the gardener, and he laid aside his livery never to resume it.

90

In the gardens he remained for a good many years, always the same, reliable in every particular, and then an uneasiness became manifest in him. When he met his master he was embarrassed, as though he had something on his mind that he wished to say, and yet shrank from saying. Then the squire received a hint that Richard wished to "have a tell" with him in private, and he made occasion for this, and opened the way. The young man still had difficulties in bringing out what was in his heart, but at last it came forth. He thought he had learned all that could be learned from the head gardener; indeed, in several points, aided by books, the underling believed he knew more than his superior, who, however, was too conservative in his habits to yield his opinions and change his practice. Richard wished to better himself. It was not increase of wage that he desired, but opportunities of advance in knowledge. He had hesitated for long, because he knew that he owed so much to his master, who had been kind to him, and thought for him for many years. For this reason he did not wish to inconvenience him, yet he believed there were many other lads in the village capable of filling his place, and the desire in him to progress in his knowledge of flowers and fruit had become almost irresistible.

When the squire heard this, he smiled. "Richard," he said, "I have been thinking the same thing. I saw you were being held back, and that is what ought not to be done with any young mind. I have already written about you to Mr. Kewe, the great nurseryman, and if he values my opinion at all and consults his own interest, by the end of the week there will be a letter from him to engage you."

Mr. Kewe did consult his own interest, and secured this young man. Then, when Richard came to take his leave, and thank his master again for his help, with heightened colour he said, "I think, sir, I ought to add that you have made two young people happy."

"Two! Richard?"

"Yes, sir. There's Mary Kelloway; she has been brought up next door to grandmother and me, and somehow we have always thought of each other as like to be made one some day, and now that I see that I am going ahead in my profession, both Mary and I fancy the day isn't so terribly far off."

"Mary Kelloway!" exclaimed the squire, and did not at once congratulate the young man.

"Yes, sir, there is not a better girl in the place."

"I am quite aware of that, Richard,—but you know——"

"Yes, sir, I know that her father and brother died of decline, and that she is delicate herself; but, sir, her mother's very poor, and more's the reason I should marry her, for then she can have strengthening things other than Mrs. Kelloway can afford to give her."

"I am a little afraid, Dick, she will not make a strong or useful wife, though that she is as good as gold I do not doubt for an instant."

"More's the reason why I should work hard with both arms and head," answered the young gardener, "and that, sir, is one reason why I have been so set on getting forward in my profession."

Richard was for a few years with the great nursery gardener, Mr. Kewe, who speedily found that nothing advanced in his favour by the squire, his good customer, was unfounded. He entrusted more and more to Richard, and the latter rapidly acquired knowledge and experience.

Occasionally, when he was allowed a day off, he would run to his native village and see his grandmother, and, naturally, Mary Kelloway. But such holidays could not be frequently accorded, for his master knew he could trust Richard, and was doubtful whom else in his gardens he could trust, and plants require the most careful watching and tending. One day's neglect in watering, one night's frost unforeseen, may ruin hundreds of pounds' worth of goods. The thrip, the mealy bug, the scale, are enemies to be grappled with and fought with incessant vigilance, and the green fly with its legions coming none know whence, appearing at all seasons, must be combated with smoke and Gishurst's compound without intermission.

One day, about noon, or a little after, a stranger came into the nursery gardens, and entering one of the conservatories where was Richard, asked if he could see Mr. Kewe.

"The master," answered the young man, "is just now at his dinner. If it be particularly desired I could run to his house."

"By no means," interrupted the visitor. "I should like to have a walk round the grounds and through the houses, and I daresay you will be good enough to accompany me. I have an hour at my disposal, and I would rather spend it here than anywhere else. I will await the arrival of Mr. Kewe."

Accordingly Richard accompanied the visitor about the nursery, and told him the names of the plants, putting aside such as the stranger ordered or selected.

"I don't know how it is," said the latter, pointing with his stick to a row of flourishing rhododendrons, "but you and all my friends grow these to perfection, whilst there is a fatality with mine; they won't flower, or if they do, they throw out sickly bloom, and the plants continually die and have to be removed."

"It depends on the soil, sir. What is your soil?"

"I don't know. Most things do well. We are on chalk."

"That is it, sir. The rhododendron has an aversion to lime in any form. A man will not thrive on hay, nor a horse on mutton chops. Each plant has its own proper soil in which it thrives. Give it other soil and it languishes and dies. Excuse me, sir, for a moment."

Richard ran to a boy who was lifting and removing a young thuja.

"Look here," he said. "My boy, when you take a baby from one room to another you do not carry it by the hair of its little head, do you? No, you put your arm under it and bear it easily—thus. You are transplanting that tree in altogether a wrong manner. You hold it—suspend it by the delicate twigs and leafage, and leave the root unsupported, dropping the soil and exposing every fibre. Treat a plant with as much consideration and tenderness as a baby, and it will thank you."

At that moment Mr. Kewe appeared, and Richard with a bow withdrew, but not before he had heard the nurseryman address the visitor as "My lord."

When Richard had gone out of earshot, the visitor, who was Lord St. Ledger, said to Mr. Kewe, "I have come here to ask you to help me. I have lost my good old head gardener. Poor fellow, he has had brain fever, and is quite beyond managing the gardens again. His head and memory are affected, and his nervous irritability make him unable to carry on smoothly with the others. I have pensioned him, and now I want another, and that speedily. I have no under gardener fit to advance into his room."

93

"You want an elderly man, my lord?"

"I want a good man, and an honest one, and one who understands the business. You know my gardens, hot-houses, and conservatories."

"If he had only been a little older——" began the nurseryman.

"Oh, I am not particular as to age."

"I was merely considering, my lord—that man who has been round the gardens with you——"

"Would suit me exactly," interrupted Lord St. Ledger. "I took a fancy to him at once. He loves plants. He looks full of intelligence and honesty."

"Honesty! Honest as the day. And as for intelligence, there is no lack of that. Experience may be wanting."

"I'll take him," said Lord St. Ledger. "I took stock of the fellow whilst he was going round with me."

"I am sorry to part with him," said the nurseryman, "and yet I should be more sorry to stand in the way of Richard's advancement."

No sooner had the young man news of his engagement, and that he had to look to a comfortable cottage, a good income, and employment in which he was sure he could be happy and give satisfaction to his employers, than he hastened to his native place, which he had been unable to revisit for six months.

He was full of hope, full of joy, but on his arrival his joy was somewhat dashed and his hope clouded. He found that his Mary, whom he had loved since boyhood, was manifestly in a decline. Hoping against hope, snatching at every encouraging symptom, she had not forewarned him, and he saw on his arrival that already she was deathstruck.

Her delicate complexion was delicate to the utmost refinement; her beautiful soft eyes were larger than they had ever seemed, even in childhood; her lovely face was lovelier than ever, with an angelic purity and beauty.

Then she told him the truth; but, indeed, he saw it for himself.

"Mary, dearest," said he, "if there is a little bit of life left only to you, let it be to me also."

"Dick, I can but be a burden."

"That—never—a joy as long as you are with me. Give me the one thing I have thought of, worked for, if it be but for a year or two."

"A year or two! Oh, Dick, only perhaps a month."

"Then let this month be our honeymoon."

And so it was.

The faithful fellow, true to everyone with whom he was brought in contact, was true to his dying love. She came, ghostlike, to church, and I shall never forget the pathos, the tenderness, the sincerity with which each took the irrevocable vows which bound in one the ebbing scrap of one life with the flowing vigour of the other.

Richard moved his frail, fading Mary to the pretty gardener's cottage at Lord St. Ledger's. There she ebbed away, happy, peaceful, with the love and devotion of her husband surrounding her.

The story of his marriage reached the ears of the ladies of the castle, and hardly a day passed without some of them coming to see her, and Lord St. Ledger gave orders that fruit and flowers were to be hers as she craved for them.

Just a month after the marriage her coffin was brought back to her native village and laid in a grave in a sunny part of the yard.

"Make a double grave," said Richard to the sexton. A double grave was made.

When the funeral was over, his old master, the squire, went to him, took his arm, and said, "Oh, Richard, you have had a terrible loss."

"I have had a great gain, sir."

"A gain!"

"Yes, sir. I could never have been happy had she not been mine. But she became mine, and she is mine—for ever."

He returned to his duties.

I have not quite done the story of Richard. For years there worked in Lord St. Ledgers woods a man, somewhat rough in manners, slow, but diligent. Only after many years was the truth known that he was Richard's elder brother. Richard had been advanced from gardener to steward of the St. Ledger estates. Faithful in his garden, he was faithful in his management of the property, and he appointed as woodman one of the same surname. It was not on account of any personal pride in Richard that the relationship was kept a secret; it was at the express wish of his brother John.

"Look y' here," said John. "You're a gen'leman, Dick, in broadcloth and silk 'at. I'm but a poor rummagy labourin' man. Now if you favours me anyway, and my lord puts me up a bit, folk 'll say, 'Oh, it's all becos he's Mr. Richard's brother.' So I reckon 'twill be best to keep that quiet, and then you can give me a leg up as I desarves it."

And John, partly by his brother's favour, mainly by his own good conduct, was advanced, but the relationship was not discovered till one day Richard was dead. He had caught a chill that settled on his chest, and hurried him off at the age of forty-five.

Then John Noble stood forward, and when Lord St. Ledger said something about Richard being laid in the churchyard of St. Ledger, then John said, "Please, my lord, no. I'm Richard's own brother, and I knowed his heart's wishes, as was told to none other. He sent for me when he was a dyin', and sez he to me, 'I've got a double grave made at the dear old home, in the churchyard, and Mary she be there, and there lay me by her. Us was together only one month, but now us shall be together world wi'out end, Amen.'"

CHAPTER XI

What a different sort of man is the village doctor of the present day from the one we can remember fifty years ago. Of course there are degrees—some able, others incompetent; some skilful, others butchers; some well-read, others with only an elementary smattering of knowledge of the healing art, and of drugs. Now, as then, there are differences and degrees, but they are not so marked now as formerly. The very able men gravitate to the towns, and there can be none utterly incompetent.

Moreover, the times are against great individuality. We in this age are all fashioned much alike; we are made as marbles are said to be made, by picking up in the rough and shaking and shaking and shaking together, till every angle and asperity is rubbed down; and we are turned out as like one another as marbles, differing only in profession, just as marbles differ only in colour.

Formerly exact uniformity in the way of thinking, speaking, dressing, acting, was not insisted upon, and the village doctor was not infrequently an oddity. He affected the oddity—to be a little rough and domineering, he put on an acerbity of manner that belied his real sweetness of temper, assumed a roughness at variance with his real gentleness of heart. Those of us who have lived all our lives in the country must look back with a smile rising to the lips, at the recollection of the village doctors we have met and made acquaintance with.

They could generally tell a good story. They were inveterate gossips—knew all the ins and outs of all the families in every grade of life within their beat, and though they kept professional secrecy, were nothing loth to tell a tale, where not within the line of professional responsibility. And they were such delightful humbugs, also, veiling their ignorance so skilfully, with much explanation in grandiose terms that meant nothing.

I remember an old village doctor who I really believe was absolutely ignorant of all methods and medicines introduced since he walked the hospitals, which was in the first decade of the present century. I have looked through his medical library since his death, I have seen his surgical apparatus, and have taken note of the drugs in his pharmacopœa, and I am quite sure that his medicinal education came to an abrupt stop about the year 1815.

He was a popular doctor, enjoyed a great reputation in his neighbourhood, maintained a large family of unmarriageable daughters, and lived in comfort in a cosy cottage embowered in elms, with its pleasant garden full of old-fashioned flowers.

This old gentleman's method, on being sent for, was at once to take a gloomy view of the case. "My dear fellow," he would say to the patient, "this is a very aggravated malady. I ought to have been sent for before. If you die, it is your own fault. I ought to have been sent for before. A stitch in time saves nine. If now, by a desperate struggle, I pull you through, then it will teach you a lesson in future not to delay sending for me till the time is almost over at which medical assistance can avail. I ought to have been sent for before."

The advantage of such an address was this. If the sick person dropped through his hands, the responsibility was thrown on the sick man and his friends. If, however, he were to recover, then it exalted the skill of the medical practitioner to almost miraculous power.

It was really wonderful how the old fellow imposed on the villagers by this simple dodge. Sometimes, after a funeral, when I have called on the bereaved, I have heard the sobbing widow say: "I shall never, never, cease to reproach myself for my dear husband's death. I feel as if I had been his murderer. I ought to have sent for Dr. Tuddlams before." If, however, instead, I called to congratulate a convalescent, I heard from him: "It is a perfect miracle that I am not dead. The doctor gave me up, but he administered what he said might kill or cure, and he is such a genius—he pulled me through. No one else could have done it, not the best doctor in London, so he told me. He alone knew and used this specific. But it was my fault leaving matters so long—I ought to have sent for him before."

After all, supposing that the country surgeon were able to set a bone and sew up a wound, it was just as well that he did not employ the astounding medicines and follow the desperate practices in force in the medical profession at the end of last century and the beginning of this. Bleeding with lancet and with leeches, cupping, cauterising, blue-pill, et toujours blue-bill, were in vogue. Starving in fever— water-gruel administered where now is given extractum carnis, toast and water in place of beef-tea—the marvel is that our forefathers did not die off like flies under the treatment.

I remember saying to a yeoman in Essex one day: "What! nine—ten miles from a doctor?"

"Well, sir, yes; it is ten. Thank heaven we all in this parish mostly dies natural deaths."

And surely, under the bleeding and salivating and starving régime, the grave had more than her due, and the doctor was the High Priest of Mors Palida, who brought to the grim goddess her victims. An old sexton at Wakefield parish church was also a headstone cutter. He was not very exact in his orthography, but he had the gift of rhyme, and could compose metrical epitaphs, that, indeed, sometimes, like Orlando's verses, either halted, or had too many feet to run on. One day he was sitting chipping out an inscription on a headstone, when the surgeon rode up. The doctor drew rein and looked at the work of the sexton.

"Halloo!" said he. "Peter Priestley, you've made a blot there," meaning a mis-spelling.

"Have I, doctor?" answered the clerk, "cover it over. I've covered over many blots o' yours." The doctor rode on without another word.

But the village surgeon had not in old days the skilled nurse as his assistant: and it is now a recognized truth that, for the sick, the nurse is more important than the doctor. He sent his medicines, but how could he be sure that they were taken, or taken regularly? The whole system of nursing was as rude as the whole system of drainage. It was all happy-go-lucky. The story is well known of the doctor sending a bottle of mixture to a sick man, with the direction on it, "Before taken to be well shaken"—and finding on his arrival that the attendant had shaken up the patient pretty vigorously before administering the draught.

The following story is perfectly true.

A kind-hearted village doctor, finding that a poor woman he was attending needed nourishing food, got his wife to send her a jelly.

Some time after he went to the cottage, found the ground-floor room untenanted, but heard a trampling, groaning, and struggling

99

going on upstairs. He accordingly ascended to the bedroom, to see a labouring man sitting on the bed, holding up the sick woman's head, whilst another labouring man—herhusband—was standing on the bed, one foot on each side of the patient, with a black kitchen kettle in his hand, endeavouring to pour the contents down her mouth. Both men were hot and perspiring freely, and the poor woman was gasping for breath and almost expiring under the treatment.

"Good gracious!" exclaimed the doctor, "what are you about?"

"Please, sir," answered the husband, blowing hard, and wiping his brow with his sleeve, "us've been giving her the medicine you sent down. It got all stiff and hard, so we clapped it into the kettle and gave it a bile, and was pouring it down my wife's throat. I couldn't hold her mouth open myself as well as mind the kettle, so I just called in my mate Thomas, to help and hold her up, and open her mouth for the kettle spout."

The life of the village doctor is a hard one. Never certain of a meal, and never certain of a sound, undisturbed sleep, he has to take his victuals and his rest by snatches, but then he inhales the fresh, pure air, and that maintains him in health. He has to keep his natural weakness and natural impatience under great control. Conceive of a man who has had several broken nights and hard days' work, with a head swimming with weariness, called in to a critical case, that he has to diagnose at once. His faculties are not on the alert, they cannot be, and if he make a mistake, an avalanche of abuse is poured down on him, whereas the fault lies not in himself, but in the circumstances.

Then, again, how vexatious, when tired out and hungry, to be suddenly called away for a drive of many miles—perhaps over the very road he has just returned along—to see a malade imaginaire, some hypocondriacal old maid, who is best dosed with a bread pill, or to attend to some pet child—whose only complaint is that it has over-eaten itself, and who is well again by the time the doctor arrives.

Then again, the accounts of the doctor are not very readily paid, often not paid till a new necessity arrives for calling him in again, and not very infrequently are not paid at all. And the surgeon cannot afford to sue for his debt in the County Court, lest he get a bad name as harsh, unfeeling, a "skin-flint."

100

The patients and their friends have odd fancies. They do not esteem a doctor much unless he "changes the medicine," that is to say, sends a pink one after one that was yellow, and one smelling of nitre after one strong of clove. But again, by a strange caprice they sometimes will have it, when, to humour this vagary, the doctor has "changed the medicine"—that this change is due to a consciousness that he has made a blunder with the yellow bottle of "stuff," and that he is going to try his success with the pink bottle. They become alarmed, think he does not understand the case, and insist on sending for another doctor. Consequently, immense tact, much humouring and adaptability, are requisite in the village doctor, if he is to maintain his reputation, more if he is going to make one. And perhaps no method is better than that of the know-nothing who said, "You should have sent for me before," and so shifted the responsibility from his own shoulders.

What scorn was poured by the doctor on the quack remedies employed by the old women of the parish! And yet, when we look back to the treatment recommended and the potions administered by the faculty in days gone by, I am not sure that the recipes of the old grandams were not the best—at least, they were harmless, and such were not the hackings, cuppings, and bleedings, the calomel, etc., of the faculty. A good many of the village remedies were charms, and charms only, and consequently rubbish.

Many years ago I remember great astonishment was caused in the more cultured portion of the congregation in our village church, by a man standing up after the blessing had been pronounced, and bawling out:

"This here is to give notice as how Sally Jago of—— parish has fits terrible bad, and as how her can't be cured unless her wear a silver ring made out o' saxpences or vourpences or dreepenny bits as come out o' seven parishes. This here is to give notice as how I be gwin' to ax for a collection at the door in behalf o' Sally Jago as to help to make thickey there ring."

In a parish I know well, but which I will not further particularize, the parish clerk draws, or did till lately, a revenue for the cure of children with fits. This was what he did; I am not quite sure that he does not do it still. He takes the child up the church tower and holds it out at each of the angle pinnacles, and pronounces certain words, what they are I have not learned. For which he receives a honorarium.

101

Now these are mere charms and are perfectly useless; they are superstitious usages, that should not be encouraged or even sanctioned. But it is quite another matter with the herbal remedies. Many of these are really useful, and a great deal more safe to take than the strong metallic poisons administered by the faculty. What an amount of mercury, in the form of blue pill, has been given to the generation now passing away! Was not grey powder much the same? Are doctors not still somewhat prone to administer calomel?

I have no doubt that many of the herbs collected and used by the old women were really effective and curative agents.

One of the plants on which greatest faith is placed is the elder. We still make elder-flower water as a cosmetic, and elder-berry wine as a febrifuge.

Old John Evelyn says, "If the medicinal prospectus of the leaves, bark, berries, etc., were thoroughly known, I cannot tell what our countryman could ail for which he might not find a remedy from every hedge, either for sickness or wound."

The borage was used for cheering depressed spirits, and we take it now in the cool tankard, with wine and lemon and sugar, not perhaps knowing why. But Bacon says that thus mixed "it will make a sovereign drink for melancholy persons."

My own experience confirms this. Good cider cup or champagne cup is sovereign against low spirits; this is due, of course, to the borage.

Where herbs are used, there is probably something valuable in their properties. The experience of many generations has gone to prove it. A workman who suffered greatly from abscesses cured himself entirely by the use of the roots of the teasel which he asked the writer of this book to be allowed to dig up in his orchard. But it is quite other with the little insects that infest the teasel head, and which are eaten to cure intermittent fevers, or enclosed in a goose quill, sealed up and worn round the neck as a preservative against ague.

A real charm is where the words are used without the medicine, and what good it can do is merely the effect on the imagination. That words alone may sometimes cure, the following story will show.

A poor woman came to the parson of the parish with the request—

102

"Please, pass'n! my ou'd sow be took cruel bad. I wish now you'd be so good as to come and say a prayer over her."

"A prayer! Goodness preserve us! I cannot come and pray over a pig—a pig, my dear Sally—that is not possible."

"Her be cruel bad, groaning and won't eat her meat. If her dies, pass'n—whativer shall we do i' the winter wi'out bacon sides, and ham. Oh dear! Do y' now, pass'n, come and say a prayer over my ou'd sow."

"I really—really must not degrade my sacred office. Sally! indeed I must not."

"Oh, pass'n! do y' now!" and the good creature began to sob.

The parson was a tender-hearted man, and tears were too much for him. He agreed to go to the cottage, see the pig, and do what he could.

Accordingly, he visited the patient, which lay groaning in the stye.

The woman gazed wistfully at the pastor, and waited for the prayer. Then the clergyman raised his right hand, pointed with one finger at the sow and said solemnly: "If thou livest, O pig! then thou livest. If thou diest, O pig! then thou diest."

Singularly enough the sow was better that same evening and ate a little wash. She was well and had recovered her appetite wholly next day.

Now it happened, some months after this that the rector fell very ill, with a quinsy that nearly choked him. He could not swallow, he could hardly breathe. His life was in imminent danger.

Sally was a visitor every day at the rectory, and was urgent to see the sick man. She was refused, but pressed so vehemently, that finally she was suffered—just to see him, but she was warned not to speak to him or expect him to speak, as he was unable to utter a word.

She was conducted to the sick-room, and the door thrown open. There she beheld her pastor lying in bed, groaning, almost in extremis.

Raising her hand, she pointed at him with one finger and said: "If

103

thou livest, O pass'n! then thou livest! If thou diest, O pass'n! then thou diest!"

The effect on the sick man was—an explosion of laughter that burst the quinsy, and his recovery.

I have said that the doctor turned up his nose at the village dame who used herbs and charms; he did not relish, either, the intervention of the Lady Bountiful, whether the squire's or parson's wife, one or other of whom invariably kept a store closet full of medicines—black draught for adults, dill-water for babies, Friar's balsam for wounds, salts and senna leaves, ipecacuanha for coughs, brown paper slabs with tallow for tightness of the chest, castor oil for stomach-ache, and Gregory's powder for feverishness.

My grandmother had such a doctor's shop, with shelves laden with bottles.

Whenever I was out of sorts, it was always pronounced to be "stomach," whereupon a great quart bottle of castor oil was produced, also a leaden or pewter spoon with hollow stem, and a lid that moved on hinges, and closed the spoon. Into this a sufficiency of castor oil was poured, then my grandmother applied her thumb to the end of the hollow handle, and this effectually retained the objectionable oil in the spoon, till this article of torture had been rammed between my teeth and was lodged on my tongue. Thereupon the thumb was removed, and the oil shot down my throat. I have that spoon now.

A servant girl was invited to a dance, and obtained leave from her mistress to go. She,however, returned somewhat early. Whereupon her mistress asked, "Why, Mary! you are back very quickly!"

"Yes, ma'm," answered the domestic with flaming cheek, "a young man came up to me as soon as I arrived and axed if my programme was full—and I—I haven't eat nothink since midday. I warn't going to stay there and be insulted."

I suppose my grandmother considered that after every great Christian festival or domestic conviviality my programme was overfull, for the leaden spoon and the quart bottle of castor oil invariably appeared on the scene upon the morrow.

On escaping from infancy with its concomitants the bottle and spoon, I fell under a greater horror still, blue pill and senna tea. My father believed in blue pill, and also believed that a cupful of senna tea after it removed any noxious effects the calomel might be supposed to leave. What a cramping, pain-giving abomination that senna tea was! As I write, the taste of it comes upon my tongue. What another world we live in, that of podophyllin pills coated with silver or sugar! How little can children of this age conceive the sufferings of their parents when they were blooming youths and maidens!

Of course, country people have got odd notions of their internal construction. A farmer's wife in Essex told me once that whenever she was troubled in her lungs she took a dose of small shot from her husband's flask. I was horror-struck. She explained: "You see, sir, my lungs ain't properly attached, and in windy weather they blows about. You know how you've got the curtain at the church door weighted with shot—that's to keep it down. Well, I takes them shot on the same principle, to keep my lungs down."

Having, at one time, a small stuffed crocodile in my room, varnished, and lodged on my mantel-shelf, I was visited by an old woman of the humblest class, about some parish pay that had been cut down by the hard-hearted guardians, when her eye rested on the crocodile, and after considering it for some time, she broke forth with, "I reckon you got thickey (that) out o' somebody's insides."

"Most assuredly not," I answered, considerably taken aback at the unexpected question. Then I added, "What in the name of Wonder makes you think so?"

"Becos," she replied, "sure enough, there's one in me, as worrits me—awful! And I wish your honnor'd go to the Board of Gardjins and take thickey baste along wi' you and show it to them gardjins, and tell 'em I've got one just the same rampaging inside o' me, and get 'em to give me another loaf, and tack on a sixpence to my pay. I'd like to keep a pig, your honnor; only how can I, when I've got a baste like that in my vitals as consumes more nor half o' what I have to eat. There ain't no offals for a porker. Can't be, nohow."

A friend of mine, a gentleman of some education, and one I should have supposed superior to such crude notions, assured me solemnly that he was acquainted with the following case:—An old dame, in a Devonshire country parish, drank some water in which was the spawn of a triton. The stomach of the good lady proved to be an

105

excellent hatching-place, and the spawn resolved into newt, which lived very comfortably in its snug, if somewhat gloomy, abode.

When the triton was hungry, it was wont to run about its prison like a squirrel in its revolving cage, only, of course, in this case, the cage did not revolve. This made the old woman so uneasy, that she was hardly able to endure it. The triton evinced the utmost repugnance to the smell of fried fish, proximus ardet Ucalegon, and it was impossible for the old woman to remain in the house where fish was being prepared for the table, as the excitement and resentment of her tenant became intolerable. My informant assured me that the old lady had applied to several doctors for relief, and had obtained none; at last she heard of a wise man, or herbalist, at Bideford, and she visited him. He recommended her to place herself under treatment by him, and to begin by starving her triton.

The patient accordingly remained in the place for three days without tasting food, enduring all the while the utmost discomfort from the exacting and resentful newt.

On the third day the uncertificated practitioner tied an earthworm to a thread and let it down the patient's throat. The triton rose to the bait, bit, and was whisked out of the woman's mouth. When she was sufficiently recovered, the herbalist showed her, in effect, a horrible monster, which he professed to have fished out of her inside. This creature was forthwith put in spirits and exhibited in a phial in the practitioner's window. There my informant had seen it—and the woman had told him her tale.

The story is well known of Dr. Abernethy and the lady who had swallowed a spider, which she said gave her great internal inconvenience. The doctor bade her open her mouth, he caught a fly, put it into her mouth, and then snapped his hand and pretended to have captured the spider which had come up her throat after the fly. The North Devon quack had played some such trick with the old woman, but with the improvement, that he had utilized the days whilst she was fasting in looking out for a live newt in a pond, and he deluded her into believing that this was the identical beast that had troubled her, and which he had so dexterously extracted.

I believe there are few parishes in England in which similar tales are not told. I remember seeing a huge oriental centipede exhibited in a herbalist's window in a large town in Yorkshire, as having been an inmate of the stomach of a human being.

106

I have heard the same story as that told me in Devon, repeated in Sussex with this variation, that instead of an earthworm tempting the newt from its retreat, a roast leg of mutton was exhibited at the mouth of the patient. A friend of mine was warned by an old woman in Staffordshire not to eat cress from a brook, on the ground that an acquaintance of hers had once thus swallowed toad-spawn which had been hatched within her.

"Look, sir, at that 'ere boy!" said an urchin to me one day; "he's gotten a live frog in his innerds, and if you bide still you can hear it quack."

"Nonsense," retorted the lad in question. "What you hear is conscience speakin'. That there chap ain't got no conscience at all. Put your ear to his stomick, and you won't hear nothin'."

The late Mr. Frank Buckland had so often heard the assertion that frogs and toads lived inside human beings, that he actually once tried the experiment on himself. He let a live frog hop down his throat. He felt no after inconvenience.

He tells a story in his Curiosities of Natural History which he received from a Lancashire man, and which agrees in some particulars with that I had from Devonshire. "There lived a man whose appetite was enormous. He was always eating, and yet could never get fat; he was the thinnest and most miserable of creatures to look at. He always declared that he had something alive in his stomach; and a kind friend, learned in doctoring, confirmed his opinion, and prescribed a most ingenious plan to dislodge the enemy, a big triton, who had taken up his quarters in the man's stomach. He was ordered to eat nothing but salt food and to drink no water; and when he had continued this treatment as long as he could bear it, he was to go and lie down near a weir of the river, where the water was running over, 'with his mouth open.' The man did as he was told, and open-mouthed and expectant placed himself by the side of the weir.

"The lizard inside, tormented by the salt food, and parched for want of water, heard the sound of the running stream, and came scampering up the man's throat, and jumping out of his mouth, ran down to the water to drink. The sudden appearance of the brute so terrified the weakened patient that he fainted away, still with his mouth open. In the meantime the lizard had drunk his full, and was coming back to return down the man's throat into his stomach; he

107

had nearly succeeded in so doing when the patient awoke, and seizing his enemy by the tail, killed him on the spot." And Frank Buckland remarks thereupon, "I consider this story to be one of the finest strings of impossibilities ever recorded." But such stories are told to this day, and believed in implicitly.

What imagination will do I can show from my own experience. When a boy, in the Pyrenees, I once drank from a spring, and saw to my horror, when I had already swallowed a mouthful, that the water was alive with small leeches. I had a bad time of it for two or three days. I firmly believed I had leeches alive and sucking my blood inside me; I felt them. I became languid. I believed they would drain my blood away. Happily, my father heard what was the matter with me, and explained to me the corrosive nature of the gastric fluid, and assured me that nothing living and of the nature of a leech could resist it. "My dear boy," said he, "from personal observation of your proceedings at meal-time, I am convinced you could digest a pair of boots, and no leeches could stand a moment against the force of your vigorous gastric fluid." I believed him, and forgot all about my imaginary malady.

CHAPTER XII

Every family and village has had its scapegrace. The family ne'er-do-weel has been its greatest curse, and has torn down and dissipated in a few years what it has taken generations to set up; any fool can destroy—only the wise can build.

But it is not so much folly as lack of principle which constitutes the ne'er-do-weel. Many a good man is a stupid one, and his goodness saves his stupidity from carrying him and his family to ruin. And sometimes a clever man is a ne'er-do-weel, because his cleverness is undirected by principle.

Perhaps the most flagrant instance of the ne'er-do-weel among the aristocracy was that of Philip Duke of Wharton, the inheritor of a princely fortune, of extensive estates, and endowed by nature with brilliant talents, a manwho forfeited everything simply because he was without principle, and died in abject poverty, the last of a race which had been the pride of the North of England; but he died in something worse than poverty—in dishonour. It was of him that Pope wrote these scathing lines:

"Clodis—the scorn and wonder of our days,
Whose ruling passion was the lust of praise;
Born with whate'er could win it from the wise,
Women or fools must like him, or he dies.

******

His passion still to covet general praise,
His life to forfeit it a thousand ways.
A tyrant to the wife his heart approves,
A rebel to the very king he loves;
He dies, sad outcast of each Church and State,
And harder still, flagitious, yet not great.
Ask you why Clodis broke through every rule?
'Twas all for fear the knaves should call him fool."

The present time shows us some of these among the inheritors of noble names and fortunes—men as foolish and unprincipled as the wretched Duke of Wharton, and who run through a hardly less disreputable course, to the disgrace of the name which has hitherto been held high in history.

In many a humbler family it is the same. It would seem as though occasionally a sport of some ignoble, sordid, selfish element broke out in a stock that has been noted for its self-respect, its goodness and generosity, and the wretched creature in which is this vein of baseness undoes in a few years everything that it has taken his ancestors many years of prudence, self-sacrifice, and forethought to construct.

The writer remembers the instance of a gentleman in the North of England of excellent abilities, of many extended estates, and of illustrious name.

He, however, had the misfortune to inherit his fortune early; he had lost his father and mother when quite a boy, and when he came into his estates he galloped through them, selling one property and mansion after another, till he came to spend his last days in a cottage.

Throughout, one had pitied the man rather than blamed him, because he had not been taught his duties to God and man at a mother's knee. But one day the writer said to him, "Well! I suppose that if we began life again, you and I, with our experiences, we should live very differently."

"Not a bit of it," he answered promptly, with a merry laugh, "I'd go through the same round to ruin again." After that, the spring of pity for the man dried up. A man who cannot learn by experience, who has no feeling for the shame and sorrow he has caused his family, deserves only contempt.

As a boy I remember seeing a painting of a young gentleman with a flat feeble face, and powdered hair, and laced coat. It was riddled with small holes. I asked the reason.

It was the portrait of the family scapegrace, who had alienated the paternal acres and mansion, and for three generations that picture had been used for the children to shoot darts at. So alone did that good-for-naught prove of the slightest use, in that to future generations he was held up as the butt of scorn and loathing in the family, as the one man who in a few years had wrecked what it had taken an illustrious ancestry many centuries to accumulate.

110

The first token of the course the scapegrace is going to take is when he begins to fell the stately trees that have been growing in his park about his estate for over a hundred years.

I will quote a scene from Coleman's capital comedy of The Poor Gentleman, which held up to detestation a man very common in that age.

"An apartment in Sir Charles Cropland's house. Sir Charles Cropland at breakfast; his valet de chambre adjusting his hair.

"Sir Chas. What day of the month was it yesterday, when I left town?

"Valet. The first of April, Sir Charles.

"Sir Chas. Umph! When Mr. Warner (the steward) comes, show him in.

"Valet. I shall, Sir Charles.

[Exit.

"Sir Chas. This same lumbering timber upon my ground has its merits. Trees are notes issued from the bank of Nature, and as current as those payable to Abraham Newland. I must get change for a few oaks, for I want cash consumedly. So, Mr. Warner.

Enter Warner

"Warner. Your honour is right welcome into Kent. I am proud to see Sir Charles Cropland on his estate again. I hope you mean to stay on the spot for some time, Sir Charles?

"Sir Chas. A very tedious time. Three days, Mr. Warner.

"Warner. Ah, good sir! I wish you lived entirely upon the estate, Sir Charles.

"Sir Chas. Thank you, Warner; but modern men of fashion find it devilish difficult to live upon their estates.

"Warner. The country about you is so charming!

111

"Sir Chas. Look ye, Warner, I must hunt in Leicestershire—for that's the thing. In the frosts and the spring months I must be in town at the clubs—for that's the thing. In summer I must be at the watering-places—for that's the thing. Now, Warner, under these circumstances, how is it possible for me to reside upon my estate? For my estate being in Kent——

"Warner. The most beautiful part of the country——

"Sir Chas. Curse beauty! My estate being in Kent——

"Warner. A land of milk and honey!——

"Sir Chas. I hate milk and honey.

"Warner. A land of fat!

"Sir Chas. Damn your fat! Listen to me. My estate being in Kent——

"Warner. So woody!——

"Sir Chas. Curse the wood! No, that's wrong—for it's convenient. I am come on purpose to cut it.

"Warner. Ah! I was afraid so! Dice on the table, and then, the axe to the root! Money lost at play, and then, good luck! the forest groans for it.

"Sir Chas. But you are not the forest, and why the devil do you groan for it?

"Warner. I heartily wish, Sir Charles, you may not encumber the goodly estate. Your worthy ancestors had views for their posterity.

"Sir Chas. And I shall have views for my posterity. I shall take special care the trees shan't intercept their prospect. In short, Mr. Warner, I must have three thousand pounds in three days. Fell timber to that amount immediately."

A singular circumstance happened some years ago. I was told it by a timber merchant who was on the spot.

A respectable nobleman died, leaving a scapegrace son to inherit his title, estates, and wealth.

112

It was then that the Jews came down like vultures on the heir. They had lent him money on post-obits; and there was not enough to satisfy them. Accordingly the mandate went forth for the cutting-down and sale of the magnificent timber in the park—trees of centuries' growth.

The day of the sale arrived, and timber merchants had gathered from far and near, and the auctioneer was about to begin the sale of the trees—standing in their majesty. "By heaven!" said the dealer to me, "it made my heart ache to see them—the trees themselves looked like nobles—I say it made my heart ache, though I hoped to profit by them too."

Well, just as the sale began a telegraphic messenger came galloping up with an orange envelope.

The earl had shot himself.

The sale was stopped. The trees could not be felled. He had cut short his own worthless life, and each stick of timber, every one of which was more valuable than his miserable self, was saved.

"As the gaming and extravagance of the young men of quality has arrived now at a pitch never heard of, it is worth while to give some account of it," writes Horace Walpole in his last journals (1772). "They had a club at one Almacks in Pall Mall, where they played only for rouleaus of £50 each rouleau; and generally there was £10,000 in specie on the table. Lord Holland had paid about £20,000 for his two sons. Nor were the manners of the gamesters, or even their dresses for play, undeserving notice. They began by pulling off their embroidered clothes, and put on frieze greatcoats, or turned their coats inside outwards for luck. They put on pieces of leather (such as is worn by footmen when they clean knives) to save their lace ruffles; and to guard their eyes from the light, and to prevent tumbling their hair, wore high-crowned straw hats with broad brims, and adorned with flowers and ribbons; masks to conceal their emotions when they played at quinze. Each gamester had a small, neat stand by him, with a large rim to hold his tea, or a wooden bowl with an edge of ormolu, to hold his rouleaus. They borrowed great sums of the Jews at exorbitant premiums. Charles Fox called his outward room, where these Jews waited till he rose, the Jerusalem Chamber. His brother Stephen was enormously fat; George Selwyn said he was in the right to deal with Shylocks, as he could give them pounds of flesh."

There is a charming old house in Throwleigh, Devon, called Wonson Manor, the ancient seat of the Knapmans, from whom it passed to the Northmores of Cleave, together with large estates in the neighbourhood.

William Northmore of Cleave, M.P. for Okehampton from 1713 to 1734, was a great gambler, and he lost at one sitting £17,000 on the turn of an ace of diamonds in a game of putt.

This led to forced sales and the loss of the ancestral acres and house of Well in South Tawton, and of nearly all the property in Throwleigh except the manor-house. William Northmore had an ace of diamonds painted in one of the panels of the wainscot of his bedroom, and every night before turning into bed he cursed the ace instead of saying his prayers. The ace is still shown. Now Wonson is also passed away.

There was in North Devon no more ancient family than Dowrish of Dowrish, whose authentic pedigree goes back to King John's reign, when Dowrish Keep was erected. The descent was direct from father to son for twenty generations, that is to say for five hundred years, always seated on the same acres and occupying the same house, that had indeed been added to, remodelled, but which was in itself a record of the lives and thoughts, ambitions, and discouragements of a family that had married into the best in the land, the de Helions, the Carews, the Fulfords, and the Northcotes.

Then, in graceless days, came the graceless fool who undid the work of twenty generations in one night. The manor of Kennerleigh belonged and had belonged to the Dowrishes for centuries.

One night the then squire and Sir Arthur Northcote were playing piquet. Mr. Dowrish, being eldest hand, held the four aces, four kings, and four queens, and promptly offered to bet his manor of Kennerleigh against £500, by no means its value even in those days, that he won the game. Sir Arthur took the bet, having a claim of carte blanche on his undiscarded hand. After Sir Arthur had discarded, he took up two knaves, and held two points of five each, each headed by the knave. Mr. Dowrish being about to declare, was stopped by Sir Arthur's claim for ten for carte blanche, which ruined his chances. The point fell to Sir Arthur, and two quints, who scored thus:

Carte blanche   10

Point   5

Two quints at 15 each	30
Repique	60
	—
	105 and game.

At the present day there would be holes to pick in this method of counting, as Mr. Dowrish on his side could have claimed his "fourteens" for aces, kings, and queens before allowing the sequences to count, but not so formerly, when the rule was absolute as to the order of counting, point, sequence, threes or fours of suits. So the manor was lost, and Kennerleigh belongs to Lord Iddesleigh at the present day.

In commemoration of the game, the table at which it was played was inlaid with representations of the two hands, and is now in Dowrish House, a mansion that has lost all its interest, having been remodelled in suburban villa style, but nobly situated and commanding a glorious view.

Gambling thus recklessly is an illustration of reversion to one of the strongest passions that actuates man in his lowest savage state. So the Alaskan natives. "They often pass whole days and nights absorbed in the occupation. Their principal game is played with a handful of small sticks of different colours, which are called by various names, such as the crab, the whale, the duck, and so on. The player shuffles all the sticks together, then, counting out a certain number, he places them under cover of bunches of moss. The object seems to be to guess in which pile is the whale, and in which the crab, or the duck. Individuals often lose at this trifling game all their worldly possessions. We are told of instances where, spurred on by excitement, a native risks his wife and children, and if he loses, they become the recognized property of the winner, nor would anyone think of interfering with such a settlement."[7]

A certain earl, when a young man, being fond of play, called on Beau Nash to gamble with him. Nash first won from him all his ready money, then the title deeds of his estates, and finally the very watch in his pocket, and the rings on his fingers—all in one night. Nash thereupon read him a lecture on his incredible folly, and returned

---

[7] Balm, The New Eldorado, Boston, 1889, p. 199.

all his winnings, at the same time extracting from him a promise that he would never play again.

But it is not among the gentry only that the scapegraces are found, though such as are highly placed are most noticed. They are to be found in every class, and there is not a village which does not produce these sour fruit.

The generality of these scapegraces are simply scatter-brains, filled with exuberant spirits that carry them beyond the bounds that constrain the commonplace folk. If these fellows, full of animal spirits, effervescing with the joy of life, have principle and wise parents to advise them, they will turn out admirable men, useful members of society. The army or the navy is the profession to which they naturally gravitate, and first-rate soldiers and sailors they make. But this is if they have principle. Without that as a fly-wheel, they spin themselves out without doing good to themselves or to anyone else.

Compare some of the scamps we have known at school, in a parish, with the heavy, plodding lout, who is without go and without intelligence. Which makes the best man in the end? The scamp undoubtedly, if his scampishness springs out of exuberant spirits and there be no root of vice in the heart.

The heavy, plodding lout becomes a wholesome and useful member of society; but he is without freshness and energy.

We cannot doubt that some untoward circumstance sometimes throws a young fellow out of his proper course of life, and throughout his career he is conscious that he has got into the wrong groove. Then he either makes the best of it, or continues in sullen resentment with resistance at heart against the restraints and contrarieties he encounters—gets into difficulties, is cast out when too late to take up another course, and squanders life away in disorder or idle repenting. I knew a boy who, getting into a "row" at school, instead of waiting and receiving his punishment pluckily, and accepting it as deserved, ran away to sea.

I met him many years after, a sailor, and he said to me, "The blot of my life was that I did not accept the birch I had deserved. I cut away to sea. I have been now a seaman for fifteen years, and have never yet found my sea-legs. Whenever there is a capful of wind, and the water is a bit rough, I am sick as a dog. It is always the same. It

116

stands against me. I hate the sea. But I made a fool of myself when I ran from school, and a fool I shall remain to the end."

"Not a bit," was my reply. "Like a sensible man, you have held to the profession you chose, and make the best of it. You win back thereby all the respect you threw away when you shirked your punishment."

There was every temptation to this young man to become a ne'er-do-weel, but he did not give way to the temptation. He recognized the fact that he had made a mistake, and he took the consequences like a man. But, then, it is, perhaps, one only in five of those who make these mistakes who has the courage to accept the results, and accommodate himself to them.

Where there is a sound substratum of healthy conscience and force of character, there one may always hope that a mistake in early life will right itself.

But if there be mere love of lawlessness, mere wilfulness, in the outbreaks of youth, then there is no redemption, the ne'er-do-weel boy remains a ne'er-do-weel to the end of the chapter.

I remember one such. I knew him as a boy, and confess to have entertained a liking for him; but his escapades passed all bounds of moderation. A good-natured, chestnut-haired boy he was, with clear, trembling blue eyes, a fair complexion somewhat marred by freckles, and straight, elastic figure. Unhappily this lad had not parents who taught their children what would do them good in life; nor kept them to the National School, where they might have acquired that which their parents neglected to inculcate.

The young fellow sometimes came to church, and then went into the gallery behind the choir. Now, in the choir sat a young fellow with a head covered with natural curls of a tow colour, on Sundays drenched in hair-oil. One Sunday the scapegrace thrust a lighted match into the mass of oiled curls, and the head blazed up at once.

The same ne'er-do-weel, whilst he was ringing the tenor bell, suddenly threw the loop of the rope over the neck of the next man, who was instantly whisked up against the belfry floor above and thrown down, and very nearly killed.

On again another occasion, he thrashed a fellow called "Old Straw" with a flail, saying that he was bent on finding if there was any good

117

to be got out of him. He broke Straw's leg, and was sentenced by the magistrates to be put in the stocks.

That was the last occasion when stocks were used in England, and so angry was the squire at the revival of the stocks, that after the sentence had been carried out he had them chopped up and burnt.

The disgrace of the stocks was too much for our ne'er-do-weel; he left the parish and entered the army, but had to leave—he was a ne'er-do-weel under the colours as in fustian. Since then he has been about the world—a ne'er-do-weel everywhere.

The other day the church bell was tolling. It was for this ne'er-do-weel. He had returned home to die. The sole wish in the heart of the man with a wasted life was to lie, to cast down the wreck of his body, in the earth of the native parish which had bred him, and to have no headstone to mark the mound under which lay naught but the ashes of a ne'er-do-weel.

CHAPTER XIII

Where there is private property there must be a demarcation, showing its limits; and where there are crops on arable land, there, either one or other of two alternatives must be adopted, the crops must be protected by a hedge, dyke, or wall, from the incursions of the cattle, or the cattle must be kept in confinement, to prevent their straying. The former is the system adopted in England and in Westphalia, and the latter is that general throughout the rest of Germany and France. The term mark has a curious history. Originally it signified the forest, so called because of its gloom, whence our word murk. The mark or forest bounded the clearing. Thence it came to signify the limit of a claim made by a community to land held in common. Land bounding a state or principality was then called also a mark or the marches, and the official who watched it against incursions was the mark-graff, or margrave, in French marquis, hence our marquess.

As the limit of a territory or a village, or a private claim had to be given certain indications, when the wood had further retreated, stones or posts were set up, and signs were cut on these to show that they limited claims. The compound was in German entitled the Gemarkung, and over every Gemarkung there was a villicus, bailiff, or schultheiss, who regulated the affairs of the community.

In 1854 Dr. Konrad Maurer set all political economists agog by his Introduction to the History of the Mark, &c. The book was not intended as a hoax, but it succeeded in hoaxing pretty largely, and in provoking considerable excitement.

His thesis was that among the Teutonic races the Land belonged to the People, and that every householder had rights over the land, but that the invasion of Feudalism altered everything, the lords then seized on the land and converted the freeholders into serfs and villains. His assertions were accepted as gospel, till disputed by Professor Fustel de Coulanges in 1885 and 1889, who showed, by production of the original texts, that Maurer had little or no evidence to sustain his entire fabric. All the evidence goes the other way, to show that land, directly men settled, became private property, but that the landlord allowed his tenants to take wood

119

from forests, turf from moors, and have certain commons for pasturage, not as a right, but as a favour.

Maurer had started from a false premise. The Mark or ager never meant common land, but the boundary of private estates.[8] In a word, as far as evidence goes, his theory was the erection of a Fools' Paradise for social and political reformers. Originally, when men were nomads, the land belonged to nobody—but when tillage began, then at once the marking out of fields became a necessity—and with the marking came proprietorship.

In France and Germany, where there are no hedges, there the properties are divided by an imaginary line drawn between two stone pegs; and as fields get divided and subdivided by inheritance, the number of these marks or pegs increases.

In order to distinguish his boundaries, a proprietor sometimes cut the outline of his foot on a slab, or took the further pains with a hammer and chisel to scoop it out.

In course of time the significance of these foot imprints in stone was completely forgotten, and as they are found all the world over, the vulgar began to regard them with awe, and create legends to account for their existence.

When Robinson Crusoe lit upon the footprint in the wet sand on the shore, he had no rest till he discovered who had left it there. And so, when the peasantry came on these marks in stone, long after such marks had ceased to have any practical significance, they cudgelled their brains to explain them, and, of course, hit on wrong explanations.

In Scotland there are several of these. So also in India and Ceylon. Buddha's footprint is venerated in five places. In the chapel of the Ascension on the top of the Mount of Olives is shown the mark of the footsteps of the Saviour. Arculf, who visited Palestine about the

---

[8] "If a proprietor encroaches on a neighbouring proprietor, he shall pay fifteen solidi.... The boundary between two estates is formed by distinct landmarks, such as little mounds of stones.... If a man oversteps this boundary, marca, and enters the property of another, he shall pay the above mentioned fine." Laws of the Ripuarian Franks, Sect. 60. So the ancient Bavarian Laws spoke of a man who took a slave over the borders, extra terminos hoc est extra marcam.(xiii. 9). See The Origin of Property in Land, by F. de Coulanges, London, 1891.

year 700, says, "Upon the ground in the midst of the church may be seen the last prints in the dust made by the feet of the Lord, and the roof is open above where He ascended." Now, however, the impress is shown cut in the rock.

At Poitiers, in the church of St. Radegund, is the footprint of the Saviour, impressed by Him when He appeared to this abbess saint.

At Bolsena is a slab on which are the footprints of St. Christina.

In Rome a chapel called "Domine quo vadis" is built over a similar slab. The story goes that St. Peter, afraid of perishing in the persecution of Nero, attempted to fly from Rome, when he met Christ at the spot where stands the chapel, and he asked Him, "Lord, whither goest Thou." "To be crucified again in Rome," was the answer. Peter, ashamed of his cowardice, returned and died a martyr's death.

In Poland as many as eighteen of these footprints have been registered.

Curiously enough, footprints outlined in the marble have been found in the catacombs of Rome closing the graves of early Christians. In the Kircherian Museum in Rome is one of these. It is a square marble slab with two pairs of footprints incised upon it, pointed in opposite directions, as if occasioned by a person going and returning, or by two persons passing each other. Another stone from the catacombs bears the name of Januaria, and has on it the print of a pair of feet in sandals carved on it.

The circumstance that all sorts of legendary matter attaches to these footprints, shows that their real significance has been lost. Yet they must have had a meaning and a purpose, and that all over the world. When the purpose for which executed no longer existed, or it was no longer necessary to express this purpose, then the purport of these marks was left to wild conjecture.

We cannot be very far wrong in saying that primarily these footprints were cut as boundary marks, or as marks indicating possession. When a settler took land and enclosed it, then he cut his mark at the corners of his enclosure; and the simplest and most natural mark was the impression of his foot.

Tin miners in old times were required annually to cut their marks in the turf of their claims. If they failed to do this, they forfeited their claims. Indeed, the very term possession is derived from the expression pedes posui—"I have set my feet down." Among the Roman lawyers the maxim held that what the foot struck that could be claimed as private property. The German word marke, marca, meant a limit, a boundary. Now we use the word mark as a sign, or token of possession. We have tradesmen's marks. And, as already said, the simplest of all marks was the footprint. If any dispute arose, the owner put his foot down on the tracing, and showed thereby a right of ownership.

We see in the footprints on tombslabs the same idea—of claiming proprietorship in a grave. The two pairs are for the husband and wife.

It has been argued that where horse hoofs have been cut in a slab, that indicates the wider limits of a domain, or a community-district, which was ridden round, but that the footprints of men thus graven betokened private lands belonging to individuals, or rather, to heads of households.

At Totnes, in Devon, in the High Street, is a slab of stone, on which is the now much worn impress of a foot. This from time immemorial has been said to have been the print of the foot of Brutus when he landed in Britain, and took possession of our Isle for himself and his descendants. As he did so he declared:

> "Here I stand, and here I rest,
> And this place shall be called Totnes!"

But now let us turn from boundaries indicated by marks to those artificially erected enclosing the entire claim.

Such are our hedges, dykes, and walls.

The hedge in many parts of England and in Scotland is a small privet or thorn division between fields, or dividing a field from the road. To a Northerner, to speak of a bank six or ten feet high with trees on the top as a hedge, is held to be a misappropriation of terms. A hedge, according to him, is only a line of quickset eighteen inches or two feet high; a bank of earth dividing fields is a dyke. But then in Ireland a dyke is both a bank and a ditch. In fact, hedge is derived from the same source as the Latin ager, and the Norse akr, and our acre; and signifies earth cast up, either by the plough or the

122

spade, either in tilling or in banking. This is the meaning the Sanskrit akara has; and in Latin, ager has its double meaning, as a bank and as a field. So I contend that we in the South-West of England are quite right in using for the banks that enclose our fields the term hedge.

It is a great hardship to the poor cattle on the Continent to be stall-fed, and how poor is the meat from such beasts every Englishman knows who has travelled. If we glory in the Roast Beef of Old England, it is because our cattle are able to roam about the pastures, and are healthy and vigorous, and their flesh sound and juicy accordingly. And this is due to our hedges.

In certain parts of the Alpine chains, there are portions delivered over to the chamois as their own, in which no gun may be fired, where the beautiful creatures may be sure of rest and security, in which they may nurture their young, and to which, when hard pressed, they may flee, as to Cities of Refuge. In Tyrol such an asylum is called a Gämsenfreiheit.

Of late years it has become necessary for law in Switzerland to extend its protection to the Edelweiss. This peculiar and beautiful flower is much in request, both by lovers whopresent it to their sweethearts, and also for the formation of little mementoes for travellers.

The Edelweiss does not require an altitude so great that it is near the snow, nor a precipitous rock to crown; the poor plant has been driven higher and ever higher, and to inaccessible points as the only places where it can live unmolested. At Rosenheim, on the Bavarian plateau, at the roots of the mountains are fields of Edelweiss, where the plant is cultivated to satisfy the insatiable visitor who insists on going home from his holiday with a tuft in his hat, and on sending dried specimens to all his friends.

Well! what must England have been before it was cultivated in nearly every part? Verily, it must have been a land of flowers. Now the flowers are banished—that is to say, the vast majority of kinds, by the plough and harrow. Only those are left which can withstand both and such as take refuge in our hedges. The hedgerow is, in fact, to our English flowers, what the Gämsenfreiheit is to the Tyrolean chamois—their city of refuge, their asylum from utter eradication.

How infinitely dreary is the landscape in France without hedges.

The eye ranges over a boundless plain of rolling land, that is divided into strips of various colours like a plaid, and no trees are visible except lines of trimmed poplars, or a scrubby wood kept for fuel. The eye ranges over belts of cabbage and colza, potatoes, beetroot, barley and lentils, wheat and sanfoin. There is not a single hedge anywhere—no harbour for such plants as have not the stubbornness to live on in spite of plough, and pick, and spade, and hoe. Flowers there are—for flowers are obstinate and persist in coming—grape hyacinths, star of Bethlehem, lungwort, scarlet anemones, tulips, blue-bottles, cornflowers, salvia, and so on—because they dive out of reach of the spade and share, or because they do not object to having their tubers cut up—they rather like it. They multiply from every portion. But this is not the case with all flowers. Some have too refined a nature, are too frail, modest, reserved, to endure rough treatment. They ask only to be let alone. They will die if incessantly worried—and for such there is no other place of refuge available except the hedgerow.

I was the other day on the battlefield of Poitiers. The chroniclers tell of the banks, the hedges and vineyard walls that stood in 1356, and afforded shelter for the English archers. Not one remains. Every hedge has been levelled, every mound spread, and with them have gone all those flowers that once made the battlefield like a garden.

Our old English hedges are the Poor Man's conservatory, are the playground of his children. How starred they are in spring with primroses! How they flush with red robin! How they mantle with bluebell! How they wave with foxglove! Talking of the latter, I was driving one day in Cornwall, when my coachman pointed to a range of foxgloves, and said: "Look there, sir! They are just like girls!"

"What do you mean?" I asked.

"Did you never notice," said he, "that the foxglove always turns its flowers towards the road—it never looks into the hedge?"

"Naturally, no flower exists that does not look to the light."

"'Tain't that," said the driver. "'Tis they know they've got pretty faces, and wants to show them."

Then, again, the ferns and the mosses! What a wealth of beauty in them! What a variety! Not to be discovered in the field; only in their own quarter, reserved for them—the hedgerow.

Our hedges are probably as ancient as our civilization. We know of a few only that have been erected within the memory of man; the majority have existed from the period when our land was first put into cultivation. And it is remarkable that in the north of Germany, in Westphalia, the Saxon region whence came our Teutonic ancestors, there the hedge with which we are familiar in England is to be met with as well, as an institution of the country, and a feature of the landscape.

Look at the size of some hedges—their width at the base, the height to which they rise, the traces they bear of venerable antiquity! This is not perhaps the case in all parts of England, but it is so in the west.

An agent of an earl, with large estates, told me that when first he took the agency five-and-twenty years ago, he waged war on the hedges, he had them swept away and replaced by low divisions with quickset over which any child might jump. But after long experience he had learned that our ancestors were not such fools as we suppose, in this matter. He learned that not only were the high hedges a protection to the cattle from wind and rain, but that they furnished a very necessary store of dry food for them at a time when their pastures are sodden. See bullocks in wet weather, how they scramble up the hedges, how they ravenously devour the dry grass in them. That is because the hedges supply them with something that they cannot get elsewhere.

In the West of England a hedge top is frequently finished off with slates that project, and this is to prevent rabbits, even sheep, from overleaping them. In Cornwall, on the bank top is a footpath beside the lane, a large deep cleft in the land, that converts itself into a torrent in wet weather. It is a common sight to see women, and children on their way to school, pencilled against the sky walking on the hedge tops. So when certain hedges have thus been converted into footways, then a rail is often put across them to prevent horsemen from using them in like manner.

Anent sheep jumping hedges, I may venture here to tell a tale of a certain old rogue who went by the name of Tup-Harry. This is how he got his nickname. Harry was a small farmer, and he had a neighbour with better means, and a better farm than his own. One very dry season Harry had come to the end of his grass for a flock of sheep he possessed. His neighbour had, however, got a fine field of mangel-wurzel. Harry looked over the hedge—a hedge furnished with outstanding slates—and greatly longed for these mangels for his sheep; but he did not relish running the risk of being caught taking them. So he went in the evening into his field that was bare of grass, put his head against the hedge, bent his back, and called "Tup! Tup! Tup!" whereupon up ran his old ram, jumped on his back, went on to the hedge, and over into the mangel field, and all the flock in Indian file scampered after him over the back of Harry. Very early in the morning the rogue went into the devastated mangel field, put his head against the hedge, bent his back, called "Tup! Tup! Tup!" and up came the ram, ran over his back on to the hedge, and returned to the barren quarter again, followed in Indian file by all the flock. That was done several times, and no signs appeared anywhere of the hedge being broken through, or of a padlocked gate having been opened. At last one night the farmer who was robbed hid himself, and saw the whole proceeding. Tup-Harry did not try that trick on again.

CHAPTER XIV

For how far down below the surface the rights of the lord of the manor extend, has not I believe as yet been determined, so we may presume that it goes down as far as man can dig and sink his shafts. In a good number of counties in England there is nothing underground worth bringing up, and consequently such rights are not of much value. It is quite otherwise where there is mineral wealth, and it is from the coal or the copper or the tin that lies deep underground that the wealth of some of our landed proprietors comes. But there is this consolation for such as have nothing of great importance below the surface, that those who are deriving their large incomes from the beds or veins deep underground are exhausting their patrimony; coal and metal will not recover themselves as the surface soil will.

It has been my lot to live where the underground industry was great, in Yorkshire where were coal-mines, and on the borders of Cornwall where were once great copper and tin mines; also in my youth manganese was extracted out of the rock on my paternal inheritance. I have had a good deal to do with those who have worked underground, and so may be allowed here to give some reminiscences connected with mining and quarrying.

Alack-a-day! As the old order changeth, one of the most fresh and delightful characters Old England has produced is disappearing. Cornish mining is almost at its end. Every week away from the peninsula goes a shipload of miners for whom their occupation is gone, and with them the old cap'n.

Well, what is our loss is others' gain! and he goes to another part of the round world to be there as a waft of fresh air, a racy and delightful companion, a typical Cornish Celt, every inch a man, strong in body, and as strong in opinions, a little rough at times, but with a tenderness of heart like that of a woman.

If we go along the great backbone of Cornwall, we find it a mass of refuse heaps—every here and there is a bristling chimney, an old engine-house, but all desolate; the chimney gives forth no smoke, the engine is silent. The story is everywhere the same—the mine has

127

failed. Is the lode worked out? Oh dear no! There is still plenty of tin—but foreign competition has struck the death-blow to Cornish mining, and the Cornish miner, if he will not starve, must seek his future elsewhere.

Of course there are captains and captains; there is the clever, wheedling captain, who starts mines never intended to pay, of which the only metal to be found is in the pockets of the dupes who are persuaded to invest in them. I knew one such. He found a mine, and was very anxious to get up a company, so he "salted" it cleverly enough, by dynamiting tin into the rock. But the mining engineer sent down to see this mine and report on it to the investors was too shrewd for him. The projected mine was not in Cornwall, but in Devon. "Halloa!" said he, "how comes this tin here? It is Cornish metal."

So that mine never got on all fours.

In a great number of cases, in the large majority, in fact, the captain is himself the dupe, and dupe of his own ambition. Mining is a speculation; it is a bit of gambling. No one can see an inch into solid rock, and no one can say for certain that indications that promise may not prove deceptive. The captain sees the indications, the dupes do all the rest. If the lode proves a failure, then those who have lost in it come down on the captain and condemn him as a rascal.

But there are cases where concealment or falsification of the truth is actually practised. Caradon Hill, near Liskeard, according to the saying, is vastly rich in ore:

> "Caradon Hill well wrought
> Is worth London Town dear bought."

It has been mined from time immemorial, but is now left at rest, and has been deserted for some years. The tale is told—we will not vouch for its accuracy—that in one of the principal mines on Caradon the miners came on an immense "bunch" of copper, and at once, by the captain's orders, covered it up and carried on their work where it was sure to be unproductive. Down, ever more downwards went the shares, as the mine turned out less and less copper, and just as all concerned in the bit of roguery were about to buy up the shares at an absurd price, in burst the water and swamped the mine. To clear it of water would require powerful

128

engines, take time, and prove costly. But as shares had fallen so low no capitalists could be found to invest, and there lies this vast treasure of copper unlifted, deep under water. "I tell the tale as 'twas told to me." Is it true? I cannot say—at all events it gives a peep into the methods by which the rise and fall of shares can be managed, and it shows how completely investors are at the mercy of the mining captains. But that there are rogues among the captains does not prove that roguery is prevalent, or that many are tainted with it. On the contrary, as a body they are thoroughly honest, but speculative and sanguine.

There is a certain captain who has great faith in the divining-rod. One day he was bragging about what he had done therewith, when an old miner standing near remarked:

"How about them eighteen mines, cap'n, you've been on as have turned out flukes?"

"I don't say that the rod tells how much metal there is, but that it tells where metal lies that is sure sartain. Now look here, you unbelieving Thomas, I'll tell you what happened to me. There was a pas'le o' fools wouldn't believe nothing about the divining-rod, and they said they'd give me a trial wi' my hazel rod; so I took it, and I went afore 'em over the ground, and at last the rod kicked, just like my old woman when her's a bit contrary. Well, said I, you dig there! and dig they did."

"And did you come on a lode, cap'n?"

"I'll tell you what we came on—a farmer's old 'oss as had been buried 'cos her died o' strangles. Well, I promise you, they laughed and jeered and made terrible fools o' themselves, and said I was done. I done! said I—not I; the divining-rod is right enough. Look, they buried the old 'oss wi' her four shoes on. The rod told the truth—but mark you, her didn't say how much metal was underground."

The endurance and coolness of the miner are remarkable. But an instance or two will show this better than by dilating on the fact.

At a certain mine, called Drakewalls, the shaft crumbled in. It was sunk through a sandy or rubbly matter that had no cohesion. When it ran in there were below two miners.

The entombment at Drakewalls took place on Tuesday, February

129

5th, 1889, and the two miners shut in by the run of ground were John Rule, aged thirty-five, and William Bant, aged twenty-one, the former being somewhat deaf. They had pasties to eat, and burnt their candles so long as they could keep them alight. They suffered most from cold and damp and want of water, their water keg being buried in the rush of sand. At one time, while they were discussing the chances of rescue, Rule said to Bant, "I believe they will come through. You never did any crime bad enough to be kept here"; to which Bant replied "No"; and Rule added, reflectively, "This would be a right place for Jack the Ripper. Us two cu'd settle'n—and ate'n too, if hard put to't." They were rescued on the night of Saturday, February 9th. The pitman, Thomas Chapman, had worked night and day without cessation from February 5th to the night of February 9th, and, moreover, was lowered eighty feet to where they were confined. None of the other men would undertake to descend, fearing lest the entombed men might have lost their reason in their long confinement. One of the most curious facts connected with the entombment was that the two men had not lost account of time, but knew almost exactly what day and hour it was. In reply to a question, they said, "It's Saturday midnight," and, as a matter of fact, it was about one o'clock on the Sunday morning.

Bant was found in a somewhat dazed condition. Not so Rule, who walked out with great composure, and the remark he made was, "Any fellow han' me a light and a bit o' baccy for my pipe?" and on reaching the grass he said, "I wonder if my old woman have got summot cookin' for me."

He was much surprised that all wished to shake him by the hand. "Why," said he, "what is all this about? I ain't done nothin' but sit in darkness."

Chapman received the Victoria medal for his devotion. He had to go up to town for it, and was presented with it by the Princess of Wales.

Very often the captains are sober, and teetotalers. But this is not always the case, unhappily; and some are temperance advocates on the platform, but something else in the public-house. There was an old chap of this description who was known far and wide for his ardent temperance harangues, and for the astounding instances he was able to produce of the judgments that followed on occasional indulgence. A very good friend one day went with him to prospect a promising new district. They entered to refresh at the little tavern, situated some twelve hundred feet above the sea, perhaps the highest planted public-house in England. The friend was amused to see Captain Jonas take the whisky bottle and half fill his glass, holding his hand round the tumbler to hide how much he had helped himself to.

"Halloa, cap'n!" exclaimed the friend, "I thought you took naught but water."

"Sir," answered Jonas with great composure, "us must live up to our elevation. I does it on principle."

Some of the Cornish mining captains have had experiences out of England as common miners. There is one I know who worked in the Australian goldfields many years ago, and he loves to yarn about those days.

"We were a queer lot," said he to me one day; "several of us—and my mate was one—(not I, you understand)—were old convicts. But it was as much as my life was worth to let 'em know that I was aware of it. There were various ways in which a score against a man might be wiped out. I'll tell you what happened once. There was a chap called Rogers—he came from Redruth way—and he let his tongue run too free one day, and said as how he knew something of the back history of a few of our mates. Well, I was sure evil would come of it, and evil did. Things was rough and ready in those days, and we'd tin buckets for carrying up the gold, and sand, and so on. Well, one day when Rogers was about to come up the shaft, by the merest chance, one of them buckets was tipped over, and fell down. I went after him down the shaft, and that there bucket had cut off half his head, and cut near through his shoulder. You wouldn't ha' thought it would have done it, but it did. Bless you, I've seen a tumblerful of water knock a man down if the water didn't 'break,' as they call it, before reaching the bottom of a deep shaft; it comes down in one lump like lead."

After a while he went on—"I had a near squeak once, the nearest I ever had. When we were going to blast below, all men were sent up except the one who was to light the fuse. Well, one day there was only myself to do it. I set fire to the fuse, and away I went, hauled up. But somehow it didn't go off. I thought that the water had got in, so before I reached the top and had got out, I signalled to be lowered again. I had just reached the bottom when the explosion took place. The rocks and stones went up past me in a rush, and down they came again. How it happened that I escaped is more than

I can tell you; but God willed it; that was enough for me. I was back with my shoulder to the rock, and the stones came down in a rain, but not one any bigger than a cherry stone hit me. But I can tell you the men above were frightened. They couldn't believe their ears when I shouted; they couldn't believe their eyes when they saw me come up without a scratch. Folks say the age o' miracles is past. I'll never say that; it was a miracle I weren't killed, and no mistake."

"Well, captain," said I, "and did you make a fortune out at the Australian goldfields?"

He looked at me with a twinkle in his eye.

"I went out with half-a-crown in my pocket. When I came back I'd got just one ha'penny."

"But all the gold you found?"

"That had a curious way of leaving me, and getting into the possession of my mate—him who'd been a convict. He grew rich, he did. I didn't. Well, I came back with experience."

"And now, cap'n, what are you going to do?"

"There's nothing going on in the old country. I'm off somewhere over the seas again. Can't help it. I love dear old England, and blessed old Cornwall above all, but if they won't or can't support me and my family I must go elsewhere."

Alas! this is too true. The mines are nearly all shut down. In one parish alone, that of Calstock, there were twenty-two in active operation a few years ago, now not one.

The miners are scattered over the world. They are gone to South Africa, to Brazil, to the Straits Settlements.

But where are no mines, there are quarries. Oh! the delightful hours spent in boyhood in old quarries! In picking blackberries where the brambles grow rank over the heaps ofrubble and ripen their delicious fruit against the crumbled stone that radiates the warmth of the sun! In groping after fossils in the chalk quarries of the South Downs, delighted in being able to extract a fossil sponge or a glistening shark's tooth!

Nothing so unsightly as a new quarry, a wound in the face of nature,

132

yet nothing more picturesque than one which is old, all the scars healed over by nature.

And then, again, what haunts old quarries are for rabbits—and therefore also places in which boys delight to spend hours ferreting Bunny.

In connexion with a quarry I will venture to tell a story—curious, because showing a form of superstition not extinct. I tell the tale my own way, but it is fundamentally true—that is to say, it is quite true that the quarryman told it; and believed himself to have been victimized in the way I relate, though I cannot vouch for the exact words he employed.

I was examining for geological purposes a quarry in Cornwall that had been opened in the side of a hill for the extraction of stone, wherewith to metal the roads. Whilst studying the strata, I observed a sort of nick in the uppermost layer of rock, under the earth which rose above the surface of the rock some three feet six inches or four feet.

The nick was about two feet deep and the same breadth, and the sides were cut perpendicularly. It was clearly artificial, and at once struck me as being a section of a grave. There was no churchyard interfered with, so that I supposed the grave was prehistoric, and at once exclaimed to the quarryman engaged in the excavation that this was a grave. He put down his pick, and answered:

"Yes, sir, it is a grave what you see here, and what is more I can tell you whose grave it is, or was. And a coorious sarcumstance is connected with that there grave, and if you don't mind sitting down on that piece o' rock for five minutes, I'll tell you all about it."

Without paying much heed to the statement that the man made, that he knew whose last resting-place it was, I inquired whether any flint or bronze weapons had been found there.

"No, sir," said the quarryman, "nothing of the sort as far as I know; it was the head of the grave we cut through, and when we sent the pick into it, the gentleman's head came down into the quarry."

"Gentleman's head? What gentleman's head?"

"Well, sir, I did not know at the time. It gave me a lot of trouble did that head, or rather the teeth from it. If you'll be so good as to sit

133

down on that stone, I'll tell you all about it, and I reckon it will be worth your trouble. It's a coorious story, as coorious a story as you have ever heard, I take it."

"I will listen, certainly. But excuse me one moment. I should like to crawl up the side of the quarry, and examine the grave."

"It's my lunch time, and I've nothing to do but to eat and talk for half-an-hour," said the quarry man, "so I'll tell you all the whole story, when you've been up and come down again. There be bones there. You'll find his neck; we cut off the head of the grave. But, whatever you do, leave the bones alone. Don't carry any away with you in your pocket, or you'll be just in a pretty way."

I made the exploration I required. I found that a grave had been cut in the rock. Clearly, when the interment took place, those who made the grave did not consider that there was a sufficient depth of earth, and they had accordingly cut out a hole in the rock, below the soil, to accommodate the dead man. Bones were still in situ. I could find no trace of coffin, but in all likelihood, if there had been one there, it had rotted away, and the gravelly soil from above had fallen in on all sides, and had taken the place of the wood as it decomposed. And if there had been a mound above the dead man, the sinking in after decomposition had caused it to disappear. There were bushes of heather above the grave, but nothing to indicate that a tomb had been in the place, as far as could be judged from above. Its presence would not have been guessed had it not been revealed by the operations of the quarrymen.

Having completed my observations, I returned to the bottom, and seated myself on the stone indicated by the workman. He occupied the top of another, and was engaged on a pie—an appalling composition of heavy pastry, potato, and bacon, grey in colour as a Jerusalem artichoke, and close in texture and heavy as a cannon ball. He cut large junks out of this terrible specimen of domestic cookery, and thrust them between knife and thumb into his mouth. As he opened this receptacle I observed that the gums were ill-provided with teeth, so that mastication must be imperfect. It is really extraordinary how the wives of working-men exhibit their ingenuity in proving "how not to do it." It is said that the way to a man's heart is through his stomach. If that be the case, it predicates either extraordinary personal fascination on the part of the wives, or really miraculous virtue on the part of the husbands, that any domestic attachment should subsist in the cottages of the agricultural labourer and artisan. Or is it that the wives are resolved to put the tenderness, the devotion of their men to the severest possible test, as cannon are run over a new suspension-bridge?

"You see, sir," said the quarryman, "when we cut that new slice we went slap through the head of the grave, and never knowed there was a grave there, till down came the head, like a snowball. It was my partner, James Downe, as was up there wi' his pick. Me was sitting here, and I'd just opened my bag for my dinner, when I heard James a-hollerin' to me to look out. I did look up, and seed that there skull come jumping down the side, and before I could undo my legs—I'd knotted them for my lunch, and had the bag open on my lap—down came the skull, and with one skip it flopped right among my victuals, and there it sat in my lap, looking up in my face, as innocent as a babe, so it seemed to me.

"Well, sir, I daresay you know, if you know anything—and you seem to be a learned gentleman—that there ain't a better preservative against toothache than to carry about a dead man's tooth in your pocket. Dead men's teeth don't lie about promiscuous as empty snail shells, and I'd often wished to have one. I suffer terrible from my teeth. I've been kept roving with pain night after night, and one ain't up to work when one has been kept roving all night, either with teeth or babies. Me and the church sexton ain't the best of friends. You see, I'm a Bible Christian and spiritual, and that there sexton is of the earth, earthy. I couldn't ask a favour of him, to accommodate me with a tooth if he haps to turn one up when digging a new grave. It is true we have got a cemetery of our own to the chapel, but it's new, and nothing is turned up there but earthworms. As this was the case I was uncommon joyful when that head came bouncing into my lap. I found the teeth weren't particular tight in, and with my knife I easily got a tooth or two out; I thought I'd be square all round, so I got out a back tooth—they call 'em molars up to the Board School—and an eye tooth and a front one. Then I thought I was pretty well set up and protected against toothache. I got my wife to sew 'em up in a bit o'silk and hung it round my neck. I may say this—from that day so long as I wore the dead man's teeth I never had a touch of toothache."

"And how long did you wear them?"

"Three days, sir."

"Not more? Why did you not retain them?"

135

"I'll tell you why, if you'll listen to me."

"Certainly. But what have you done with the skull?"

"Chucked it away. It weren't no good to nobody—least of all to the owner. And for me—I'd got out of it all I wanted."

"You have not the teeth now?"

"No. I kept them for three days and then chucked them away."

"Have you had toothache since?"

"Terrible; but I had what was wusser when I had the teeth."

"Well, go on and tell me what the wusser was."

"So I will, if you'll listen to me. Well, sir, I had them teeth done up in a bit of silk, and hung round my throat. The first night I went to bed, that was Saturday, I had the little bag round my neck. I hadn't laid my head on the pillow, before—but, I must tell you, I'm a Bible Christian, and a serious man. I'm a local, I am, and I preach in our chapel, and am generally reckoned a rousin' sort of a preacher. For, sir, I knows how to work 'em up. Well, when you understand that, you will comprehend how astonished I was when I laid my head on the pillow, to find I wasn't no more what I ought to ha' been. In the first place, I hadn't gone to bed in my clothes, and no sooner was my head on my pillow than I was in a red coat and breeches and gaiters; and what is more, in the second place, I'd laid me down to rest, and I found myself astride on a saddle, on horseback, tearin' over the country, jumpin' hedges, tally-hoin'—me, as never rode a hoss in my life, and never tally-hoed, and wouldn't do it to save my soul. I knowed all the while I was doing wrong. I knowed I'd got to preach in our chapel next evening, the Sabbath Day—and here was I in a red coat, and galloping after the hounds, and tearin' after a fox, and swearing orful! I couldn't help myself. I believe my face was as pink as my coat. I tried to compose my mouth to say Hallelujah, but I couldn't do it—I rapped out a—but, sir, I dussn't even whisper what I then swore at the top o' my voice; and I had to preach at a revival within some few hours. It was terrible—terrible!"

I saw the quarryman's face bathed in perspiration. The thought of what he had gone through affected him, and his hand shook as he heaved a lump of pasty to his quivering lips.

"I tried to think I was in the pulpit; you must understand, sir, if at a right moment you bang the cushion and kick the panels—it'll bring down sinners like over-ripe greengages. But it wor no good; I was whacking into my cob, and kicking with spurs into her flanks, and away she went over a five-barred gate—it was terrible—terrible, to a shining light, one o' the Elect People, sir,—such as be I."

The man heaved a sigh and wiped his brow and cheeks, and rose with his pudding-bag.

"All the Sabbath day after that," continued the quarryman, "I wasn't myself. It lay on my conscience that I'd done wrong; and when I preached in the evening there was no unction in me, no more, sir, than you could have greased the fly-wheel of your watch with; and usually there's quite a pomatum-pot full. I didn't feel happy, and it was with a heavyheart and a troubled head that I went to bed on the Sabbath night." He heaved another sigh, and folded up his lunch-bag.

"Will you believe it, sir? No sooner had I closed my eyes than I was in a public-house. I—I—who've been a Band of Hope ever since I was a baby. I've heard say I never took to the bottle even in earliest infancy, though it was but a bottle of milk, so ingrained in me be temperance principles. I've heard mother say she put a bit of sopped bread into a rag, and let me have that when a baby—so stubborn was I, and so furious did I kick out with my little legs when shown the bottle. It was the name, I reckon, set me against it. However, sir, there I was, just out of the pulpit at Bethesda, and in the 'Fox and Hounds' drinking. I tried to call out for Gingerade, but the words got altered in my throat to Whisky Toddy. And what was more, I was singing—roaring out at the top of my voice—

> "'Come, my lads, let us be jolly,
> Drive away dull melancholy;
> For to grieve it is a folly
> When we meet together!'"

The quarryman covered his eyes with his hands—he was ashamed to look up.

"If that wasn't bad enough, the words that followed were worse—and I a teetotaler down to the soles of my feet.

> "'Here's the bottle, as it passes
> Do not fail to fill your glasses;

137

Water drinkers are dull asses
When they're met together.

"'Milk is meet for infancy,
Ladies like to sip Bohea;
Not such stuff for you and me
When we're met together.'

"All the while I sang it I knew I was saying good-bye to my consistency, I was going against my dearest convictions. But I couldn't help myself, it was as though an evil spirit possessed me. I was myself and yet not myself. It was terrible—terrible—terrible!"

The quarryman swung his pasty bag and smote his breast with it.

"That warn't all," he continued, and lowered his tone. "There was an uncommon pretty barmaid with red rosy cheeks and curling black hair; and somehow I got my arm round her waist and was kissing her. Well, I don't so much mind about that, for kissing is scriptural, and Paul calls them kisses of peace. But these were not kisses of peace by any means—and there was the mischief, for I knowed my wife was looking on, and, sir, I knowed the consequences would be orful—orful—simply orful."

The quarryman's head sank on his knees, he clasped his hands over the back of his head, and groaned for full five minutes. Presently he looked up, pulled himself together, and continued his narrative.

"The worst of all is behind. I was very busy on Monday, as I was on Mr. Conybeare's committee. We were in for the election, and I'm tremendous strong as a Liberal, and for Home Rule, and I reckon I can influence a good many votes in my district of Cornwall. Well, sir, I'd been about canvassing for Mr. Conybeare very hard, yet all the while I had a sort of deadly fear at my heart that what I'd been doing, both hunting and drinking, and swearing and singing, and kissing the barmaid, would come out in public, or would be thrown in my teeth by the Consarvatives, and might damage the good cause. But no one said nothing about it on Monday, and towards evening my mind was more at ease.

"I was very tired when I went to bed, for I had been working, as I said, very hard indeed, and persuading of obstinate politicians is worse than breaking stones for the road, and far worse than converting of obstinate sinners. No sooner had I laid my head on

138

the pillow than—will you believe it, sir?—I was in the full swing of the election. I didn't know it was coming on so fast. I thought it would be three weeks, but not a bit of it. They'd set up a polling place in the Board School, and there was I swaggering up to register my vote. There were placards—Unionist on one side, but I wouldn't look at them; on the other were the Radical posters—from Mr. Conybeare—and I knowed my own mind. If any man in England be true and loyal to the G.O.M. that's me. Well, sir, in I walked and gave my name. I knowed my number, and went as confident as possible into the little box of unplaned deal boards, and with my paper in one hand took the pencil in the other, wetted the pencil with my tongue to make sure it marked black enough, and then set down my cross. Will you believe it?—that sperit o' pervarsity and devilry had come over me once more, and I'd gone and voted Consarvative."

The quarryman staggered back, and I had just time to spring to his aid. He had fainted. I held him in my arms till he came round. I threw water over his face, and by degrees he was himself again.

"Orful! orful! wasn't it?" said he. "Well, sir, after that I would have nothing more to do with them teeth. They did it. I chucked 'em away; toothache would be better all night long, than the trials I had to undergo when I had them dead man's teeth about me."

"But have you not dreamed since?" I asked, looking at the pasty which, when he fainted, I had taken in my hand.

"Yes, sir, often, very often; but then my dreams since have always been Nonconformist, Temperance, and Radical dreams—and them's wholesome."

"You said something about knowing who it was whose grave you had disturbed?"

"Well, so I believe I do. I did not know at the time, but afterwards, when I began to tell my story; then there was a talk about it and a raking and a grubbing among old folks' memories, and there was an old woman who said she could throw some light on the subject. Her tale was that about a hundred years ago, or more perhaps, she could not be sure, there lived at the Old Hall one Squire Trewenna. The Hall has been pulled down because of the mines, and the Trewennas are all gone. Squire Trewenna was a terrible man for hunting and drinking, and was, moreover, a regular rory tory Conservative. He

139

was a fast chap, and no good to nobody but to dogs and horses, and before he died he begged that he might be buried on the brink of the moor where he'd ridden so often and enjoyed himself so much, and had killed a tremendous big fox in the last hunt he ever went out in before gout got to his stomick. And he said he wanted no headstone over him, that fox and hounds and horses might go over his grave. Well, folks forgot, as there was no headstone, where he lay, exact, and old Betty Tregellas says she believes what we cut into was Squire Trewenna's grave. I think so too, for how else was it that when I had those teeth about me I was so possessed wi' a spirit of unrighteousness and drinking and Consarvatism? I reckon you've had a Board School education and been to the University, and are a larned man. Tell me, now, am I not right?"

www.ingramcontent.com/pod-product-compliance
Lightning Source LLC
Chambersburg PA
CBHW011513170626
46810CB00009B/3350